HOMESICK

HOMESICK

M. Ruggiero

iUniverse, Inc.
New York Lincoln Shanghai

Homesick

iUniverse, Inc.

For information address:
iUniverse, Inc.
2021 Pine Lake Road, Suite 100
Lincoln, NE 68512
www.iuniverse.com

ISBN: 0-595-31819-3

Printed in the United States of America

Good creatures, do you love your lives
  And have you ears for sense?
Here is a knife like other knives,
  That cost me eighteen pence.

I need but stick it in my heart
  And down will come the sky,
And earth's foundations will depart
  And all you folk will die.

—A. E. Housman

Contents

Crossing the Bar

Richard Coltello stared at his shoes. They were nice shoes, he thought. Patent leather. Tassels. Not to be vomited on. Sliding them out of the way, he pushed forward and heaved. Nothing. Again. He lit a cigarette, choked, got rid of it, and proceeded as planned across Passyunk Avenue. At the corner of the street, he entered Molly's and was greeted at the door.

"Molly's Bar and Grille" does not serve food; the fabled grille of its name-sake along with its more sophisticated, and, for all that, decidedly wrong spelling were strictly ornamental, the residue of Geno Imperato's good intentions when purchasing the place. Molly's was named after Geno's second wife, who, unlike his first, allowed herself to be beaten into the floors of the above apartment as small payment for the considerable prestige.

On a usual day, full houses lost to fours of a kind, cue balls caromed out of corner pockets, thoroughbreds ran circles across the televisions screens, and Sinatra crooned from the jukebox of chewing it up and spitting it out. The walls were a standard montage of Joe DiMaggio, Rocky Marciano, Vito, Sonny, Michael Corleone, and Robert De Niro-as-Jake LaMotta-doing-Marlon Brando-as-Terry Malloy, all of whom the patrons believed (fictional status not withstanding) to have come of age in the same South Philly neighborhood as Mario Lanza during one legendary and fecund period of Italian Renaissance.

"Look who it is!…Richie Knife! Where the hell you been? Jimmy, get Richie a drink, will ya? On me."

Jimmy complied, scooping ice into a glass. "How ya doin', Rich?" he asked.

"Couldn't be better."

"Good to hear."

Richard nodded a "thank you" from across the bar; it was unusually empty. Besides the bartender and himself, two others were seated in conversation: the man responsible for Richard's drink, a.k.a. "The Frog," so named, of course, for his voice, which sounded like something filtered up from the bottom of an aquarium, and an old man of no less than ninety, sucking for dear life on a rotten cigar, known only as "Manigut" for reasons unknown, but most likely having to do with an incident occurring some sixty-seven years ago, when he made the life-altering decision to order that particular pasta an impressive three nights in a row.

The Frog, white-haired and huge, was belly beneath his chin, and belly above his knees—a giant globe of a belly—around which stretched some sixty-seven inches of belt like an equator sailed by a silver, steamship buckle struggling against imminent wreck. He was a disabled roofer, whose colon, on an atypically slow day, and tired of all these, had exploded into his stomach, earning him the alternate nickname "semicolon" among friends. He was, like the bugs, a permanent fixture in Molly's and just about everywhere else. One day, perhaps, he would listen to the same speech from Dr. Cassavetti as Richard had. Today, perhaps, Richard would set an example.

Manigut, on the other hand—and God bless him—had the life expectancy of Tithonus. Because of either the weight of his glasses, fishbowls being bench pressed by a colossal squash of a nose, or his "lucky" *Caesar's Palace* tie, hanging low enough to peep between his legs, or, being a poetic soul, his heavy heart, he sat stooped on his stool, listening to the conclusion of a story as told by The Frog:

"Mikey takes off for the door, right? *He don't wanna hear nothin'!* He's got his one arm out, ready to push it open, when somebody *pulls* it open from the outside! He goes flyin' out the door, into the street, and winds up gettin' himself hit by a van! God's honest truth! Spun him around and left him on the sidewalk! So I run outside, help him up, the whole bit. He's perfectly fine, but he's got this big, black smudge on the front of his suit, right? And this thin red welt down the center of his face…From the aerial of the van! I swear to God! Whacked him right in the face! I start wipin' him off, you know, fixin' him up, when this old lady comes to her door, real concerned, and asks, "Is he okay? What happened to him?" So I say, and I can't tell ya how I thought of it, I say, "Madam, my dear, this man has a sickness…a disease, if you will…*A van-aerial disease!*"

Manigut, God bless him, lost his cigar smoke, and nearly his teeth, and nearly his ghost, as he lurched more dangerously forward in a fit of coughing, which, as is usually the case among the ancient, had usurped the role of laughter.

"Take it easy, will ya?" The Frog said. "It wasn't that funny, geez…You even know what I'm talkin' about?"

Manigut recovered, reached into his pocket and unfurled a hanky across the bar, revealing an extensive collection of pills, varying in color, size and shape.

"Must be lunch time," The Frog said. "What are you on a picnic? Jesus Christ!"

The old man waved him off.

"Yo, Rich, take a look at this. He's got a drug store over here. Whattaya need?"

"Nothin' Frog, thanks. I'm good," Richard answered.

The Frog turned his attention to Richard, leaving Manigut to stuff his face in peace. The Frog eyed him seriously. Richard felt like he was wearing his liver on his sleeve.

"So how you been, Rich?" The Frog asked.

"All right."

"What's new?"

"Nothin' much."

"I hear that. Same old, same old, huh?"

"Yeah, you know."

"The senior citizen over there got you a drink, right?"

"Who?"

"Go ahead, Jim, tell him."

"Shut up Frog," Jimmy said.

"No? Then I'll tell him. Guess who got a senior citizen discount this morning?"

"Goddammit Frog!" Jimmy exploded. "I'm fifty-two years old!"

"You wish! Fifty-two," The Frog said. "You make 'Gut here look like a friggin' toddler, and believe me, he don't need nobody's help now they got him wearin' them diapers. Ain't that right, 'Gut, they got you wearin' diapers?"

Manigut nodded.

"It's my moustache," Jimmy said, turning to Richard. "I gotta shave my moustache, Rich."

"Yeah, that'll help!" The Frog continued. "You gonna shave them wrinkles, too? Look like a bloodhound! Here boy, here!" He clapped his hands and whistled, elbowing Manigut for support. The old man grimaced and plunked another pile of pills into his mouth.

"You old junkie, you! Be careful with that, will ya? You're liable to croak wit all them pills. Hey, he's liable to croak!" The Frog said with genuine alarm, pointing at Manigut.

"Then let him croak! And you can join him," Jimmy said.

"Me? You're the only other senior in here. Anybody else is dyin' it's you!"

Jimmy bit his fist to keep from screaming.

The Frog shook his head at Manigut. "How the hell'd you last so long?" Manigut, oblivious when he chose to be, simply snorted and washed the pills away with his beer.

Upstairs, Geno and Molly began to argue.

"There they go," Jimmy said. "I feel bad for Geno. The bitch never stops."

"It ain't her fault," The Frog said valiantly.

Richard yawned and stirred the drink untouched before him. His desire for it was useless now; it could do nothing more than gnaw at and further corrugate the edges of the hole in his stomach. His body would rebel against it at the taste and cancel it in blood. Besides, he was sick with medication. He sat there and inhaled it.

"Jimmy," he called his bartender. "Where is everybody?"

"I don't know. It's early yet."

Annoyed, Richard watched South Philly flounder on through the open blinds of the window, trying to avoid eye contact with the mirror behind the bar. Outside, a policeman, fearing imminent fire, was giving a parking ticket to a car parked in front of a plug, as passing drivers, seeing his momentary distraction, slid contemptuously through stop signs. Richard fixed his gaze on the betting odds flashing on a TV set perched atop a refrigerator. *You Belong to Me* by The Duprees played on the jukebox. Richard drummed the bar with his fingers.

"Hey, Jimmy, com'ere for a second," The Frog, inspired, signaled to his bartender.

"I been askin' Gut over here, but he don't remember. Old bastard don't remember yesterday. Wait a minute, how old are you now, Jim? Seventy-five? You never know, you know? You mighta got the old-timers, too. When's your next check-up?"

"Frog, I'm tellin' you, Frog, one more time…I'm fifty-two and you know it."

"Really? You look older. Anyway. I was just wondrin'. Do you, by any chance, remember your first blow job? Go 'head, take your time."

Jimmy answered that yes he did indeed remember the first time, and, raising his eyes to the rafters, came awfully close to reliving the experience, shaking his head and saying with a sigh, "Down by that basement entrance, over there by the church at Saint Matthew's, remember? Remember that stairway? Best of my life, Frog, the best of my life. But ain't it always the first time's the best?"

"Sure it is, but here's the thing," The Frog continued, gurgling amphibiously at the prospects of a punch line. "Do you, by any chance, happen to remember your *fifth*?"

Manigut, visibly shaken, teetered on the brink of eruption, coughs already sneaking out his nose.

"My fifth?" Jimmy squinted through hundreds. "Nah, not off-hand, Frog."

"Why not!" The Frog shrieked. "Didn't they all taste the same!"

Manigut's enraptured heart must have momentarily stopped, for he was frozen solid. The glee caused by Jimmy's humiliation had crippled him. His eyes were bulging behind his glasses and he appeared to be changing colors. The Frog wondered aloud if, mother of mercy, this was indeed "the end of Rico," and whether or not he should "call the paramedics." Richard imagined the tangled coughs traveling in knots up the old man's chest like food traveling down the body of a snake, when, finally, they came, and Manigut was in ruins.

As The Frog impressed upon his friend the need for and the downright importance of a drink of water, the phone rang.

"Molly's. Right." Jimmy hung up, and projecting his voice over Manigut, addressed the bar. "Nine, Goddammit!"

The Frog was outraged. He closed his thumb and first two fingers like a priest offering communion and shook them at Manigut. "Nine!" he screamed. "What'd I tell ya? You old bastard! I listen to you! 'Bet four'! Nine! Nine, that's my number!"

The old man coughed in rebuttal, still trying to piece himself together.

Jimmy stuck his face between them. "Come to think of it Frog, my fifth was—"

"Shuddup and get me a drink…I knew it was nine."

Richard stood up and worked his way to the men's room. The stench was palpable. He stood before the urinal, held his breath and bit his lip. He opened his eyes and paid attention when he heard The Frog give his customary greeting:

"Look who it is! The skinny guinea with the ravioli eyes! Where the hell you been? Jimmy, get Tommy a drink, will ya? On me."

Richard tucked his shirt in hastily and turned to the sink. He paused in front of the mirror, smiling. His heartbeat hurt. A certain idea, the reality of which had seemed so many times to be out of his hands, would at last today be brought into being by them. "Most people go skydiving," he thought and laughed. Drying his hands, he exited the men's room and took a seat next to "Tommy," who gestured something like hello in his direction.

Richard and Tom had known each other since childhood, had lived four doors apart. Tom still, in fact, lived on the same street in the same house with the same mother, who was very sick and nearly dead. He was deceptively handsome. He was, if not the proud owner, then the owner nonetheless of the largest pair of ears since Midas made an ass of himself, the lobes of which, Richard claimed, flapped like flags when Tom stood still in the wind. He had a flat face and a square head, made three dimensional by a crescent shaped chin and a nose more like a snout situated somewhere between his red and yellow "ravioli" eyes. But what had always irritated Richard most about Tom were his awful teeth. They were crooked and crowded, jutting in every direction, at every angle, preventing Tom from closing his mouth. Richard hated them.

Tom opened his newspaper in front of a well-worn, overexerted *Kill Mumia* tee shirt. "First number come out yet?" he asked.

"Nine," Richard answered.

"Nine! Again? The sonovabitch. That's three days straight it opens nine."

Tom pointed at The Frog, who was standing at the entrance of the men's room giving Manigut the tail end of a stern lecture.

"I know them two dopes down there didn't hit. Did yous?"

Richard and Jimmy, to Tom's relief, both admitted they had not.

"Man, I can't hit for nothin' no more," Tom said.

"Me neither," Jimmy said.

"What's the use? It's like my father used to say to me: 'If you learn somethin' after dyin', it's that you shoulda done it sooner.'"

"Amen," Jimmy assented. "So what happened? Yous ever make it to the casino last night or what?"

Tom shook his head. "Nah, got back too late. Ran into some trouble over at the strip joint."

"With who?"

"Nobody. Three niggers. Bobby got a little too close to one of the girls. I don't know."

"Ain't you supposed to get close to the girls?"

"Yeah, well, it was some black broad. I think it was one of their girlfriends or somethin'."

"What happened?"

"Nothin'. We went outside."

"That's it?"

"No, that's not it. Will ya gimme a chance? The first one, he gets in Bobby's face and says, 'you got a problem?' And the second one, he steps in and says, 'we can settle it right now.' And you know how they talk. So Bobby punched the third one in the mouth before he could open it."

"No way!"

"Yep. Cops came and everything."

"Yous got arrested?"

"No, they sent us home. They took the niggers."

"Just them?"

"Yep."

"Good to hear," Jimmy said. "That reminds me. What's the worst thing you can call a black guy that ends with an N, I mean, that begins with an N and ends with an R?

"Too easy," Tom said.

"No, no, no. Think about it. It ain't what you think."

Tom shrugged. "If it ain't a nigger then what?"

"Your neighbor!"

"Ha! That's good! That's good. My street's still clean, though, knock on wood." Tom knocked on the bar.

"Yeah well, I got about five on mine. Fuckin' disgrace."

"Tell me about it."

"Tom?" Richard broke in.

"What?"

"Can I talk to you for a minute?

"About what?"

"Nothin'. I gotta tell ya somethin'."

"Then tell me."

"Can we get a table?"

"What's wrong with right here?"

"Nothin'. It's personal."

"Jesus, Rich, what is this? First you'll want a table then you'll want a room. I just got here for Christ's sake. Can't I finish my drink?"

"Five minutes, that's all."

"Five minutes. Hold on, let me make a call first. Jimmy, gimme change for the phone. I'm bound to hit this number."

Tom gathered his quarters and left for the phone. Richard ordered a water.

"Water? Why don't you just drink what's in front of you? There's more water in it than whiskey now."

"Will you please just give me a water?" Richard said. "I'm not drinking."

"Not drinking? What are you drunk?"

"Please!"

"All right! Calm down!"

Jimmy gave him a glass of water.

"Thank you," Richard said, watching Tom flail at the telephone, until his view was eclipsed by The Frog, who had emerged from the men's room and who was having a lousy time guiding his buckle back to sea.

Tom, doing his best Magellan, circumnavigated The Frog and returned to his seat. Forgetting Richard's request, he sipped his drink while reading the obituaries.

"Tom?"

"What? Oh right, your little conference. Make it fast, c'mon."

Richard and Tom crossed the bar past the pool table and sat alone by the entrance to the kitchen, home of the infamous, dysfunctional "grille."

"Yeah, what is it?" Tom said.

"How'd it go last night?" Richard asked.

"Where?"

"At the casino?"

"At what casino? I just told you, we never made it."

"That's right! The fight and everything. I'm sorry."

Tom looked at his watch. "You got somethin' to tell me?"

"Yeah. I heard you came into some money...Is it true?"

"Little bit. My uncle, he...Why?"

"Heard it's more than a little. Must have big plans, huh?"

"Not really."

"New car, new clothes?"

Tom was silent.

"C'mon. You gotta buy a new car, right? I mean, you've had that Lincoln out there now for how long?"

"Why you wastin' my time, Rich?"

"Plan to travel?"

"Jesus Christ! How the hell do I know?"

"I'm just wondrin'."

Quat! Quat! Quat! Quat! The Frog's voice boomed in the background. He and Manigut were playing *Morra* in Italian for next drink.

"Look, I ain't got no money for you, if that's what this is about," Tom said.

"No, it ain't that. I don't want your money, don't worry."

"Then what? Spit it out! I got things to do."

Say-eeeeeeee!

"How's your mother?" Richard asked.

"My mother? What's she got to do with it?"

"Can't I ask?"

"She's drivin' me crazy. I wish she'd hurry up and get it over with."

OttoOttoOttoOttoOtto!

"Will you listen to that dope? Why they gotta play so loud? He knows he throws five everytime."

Richard ignored him. "She's that bad, huh?" he asked.

"Who? My mother? Yeah, she's like you."

"Like me?"

Traaayyyy! Tray! Tray!

"Yeah, like you. Everybody knows you're sick, Rich. Who you foolin'? You ain't been around for months."

"I never told anybody," Richard said, hesitating. "They knew?"

Do-way! Dooo-way!

Tom shook his head at The Frog. "Of course they knew. We all knew. Jesus, Rich, have you seen yourself? What the hell you doin' here anyways?"

Richard stared at his shoes.

"Is that all? Can I go now?" Tom said after a moment.

Quat! Quat! Quat!

"No, wait…I gotta ask you somethin'," Richard said absently.

"What? How my mother's doin'? You just did."

Chinnn-kwaaaaaah!

Richard straightened. "I could care less about your mother," he said.

"Excuse me?"

"Forget it, listen—"

"Watch yourself, Rich. I don't care how sick you are."

"Sure you don't."

Sett-uh! Sett-uh! Sett-uhhhhhhh!

"You got nerve," Tom said. "Whatta you think? You're dyin' now, you can say whatever you want?"

"I can *do* whatever I want," Richard said, standing. "Listen, Tom, you think maybe you could shut up for just a minute? And could you try to sit still, please? I'm about to shoot you in the mouth."

Tom smiled. "Rich, what are you—"
"Nonono, don't move," Richard said. "Just like that stay."
No-vaaayyy! No—

Consummatum Est

Here's how it begins: I was drinking in the closest bar corrupt enough to serve me. I was younger, then, and underage. Lord knows, I wasn't there by choice. It was the type of place the most devoted naturalists steer clear of. And one of many in the mess hall I called home.

I spoke as little as possible, preferring instead to observe and to listen to the drunks and their conversations (being a sort of naturalist myself). Every so often I was asked to assist one of them with a question at the trivia machine, which had been installed, much to their perplexity, in the corner of the bar. They called for me in times of difficulty, you see, because I had acquired a reputation, along with its accompanying stigma, as a "reader." Something like this:

"Quick! What was Shakespeare's shortest play?"

"I told you last night."

"But I forget. Quick!"

"Timon of Athens."

"That's not a choice!…Hurry up!"

"King Lear."

"Thanks!"

In time, when their indignation ceased to amuse, I trained them to stop asking. "You shouldn't forget," I told them. They never remembered.

I circled the room with my eyes, turning my attention to one patron in particular. He was standing in the doorway of the men's room, counting money, making plans. He retreated to the phone by the dartboard, encouraging an errant toss to the left. I watched as he dialed, wondering what kind of person would answer phone calls from him, and guessed at his whereabouts come closing time.

His name was George Lestin. He was twenty-two, the son of a junkie mother three years dead and a junkie father still alive, in theory, and living on the street. George himself lived with a cancer-livered grandmother, whose painkillers he robbed and sold and used. He would give her just enough to keep her quiet, but not always. Neighbors sometimes fell asleep to the sound of her writhing.

He had the face of a rottweiler crossed with an imbecile, its features centered around a shriveled, half-eaten nose, reminding me of those sported by the syphilitic rakes in a Hogarth engraving. His skin was disastrous, pockmarked and pimpled, like a field of active and detonated mines. Puberty had landed, spiked its flag and decided to stay, establishing a budding metropolis upon his forehead's *terra firma*. It comforted me to think that a parent's curse had fretted those channels in his cheeks, that some twisted, Dorian Gray-like pact, where nothing remained beautiful, nothing remained young, had cursed him to disclose the shredded state of his parents' veins. There was simply no rational explanation for so much ugliness. In short, he was irredeemable, was both the insect and the refuse.

But here is the astounding part! Do you know that at that moment I pitied him, that I exonerated him, that I blessed him unaware? Yes, that a spring of something close enough to love gushed from my heart—and I blessed him unaware? Could he be blamed, after all, for the fatal half-heartedness that had willed him to the world? Or for the sin and death that met him at the exit of the womb? I admit that I was seized, yes, *seized* with *compassion* for him, and forgave him everything.

His future played out before me. He would, had he not already, draw a young girl into his mud, molest her soul, break her to pieces, and walk away from it unscathed, and get away with it forever. He would reproduce another like himself, equally cursed at conception, and the downward spiral, swirling in its own disgust, would continue its dizzying descent. Was the bottom in sight? Still, I pitied him—from a distance, you understand—and afterward returned him to the property and problem of others.

My thoughts were disturbed by the front door. A man entered and asked if I would be interested in purchasing for five dollars a lighter that, at the push of a button, doubled as a switchblade. I held my breath.

He appeared to be covered in ashes, as though a fireplace had coughed on him, or as though he had taken to testing his lighter on himself. There were holes in everything from his sneakers to his tee shirt to his face. It was George's father. I acted as if he had offered just the item I'd been clamoring for, and bought it, I supposed, to clear my conscience of human beings.

George noticed him and was furious. He charged at his father from across the bar, grabbed him by his throat and threw him against the cigarette machine, screaming in that stoned, illiterate lisp of his, "What I tell you 'bout botherin' my friends, Dad, huh? What I tell you?"

George's father took a broken nose to the floor with him and squirmed to a series of kicks in his back. He was in the fetal position when George brought the legs of a bar stool down on his shoulders. Father and son were bonding at last. It was enough to make Turgenev cry.

The two were separated, or George was pulled off, and both were escorted outside. While George was detained, his father made off to wherever with my money in his pocket. I remember hoping he'd overdose and remember reprimanding myself. But did these people have a right to life? I couldn't answer then, though I was embarrassed by my earlier sentiments. Someone handed George his jacket, telling him to avoid the bar, to which he objected mildly before giving up and moving on.

Inside again, I ordered a final drink and watched the men beside me, who, having been stirred by the unexpected outburst of violence, had begun to arm wrestle. It was the final blow to my already dwindling sense of self-respect, and, hoping to salvage what was left of my dignity, I finished my drink, left the lighter/switchblade for the bartender (it was worth at least five bucks), and said my farewells with an all-encompassing and scarcely noticeable wave goodbye. There had been enough excitement for one night and I was tired of everything but sleep.

I reviewed the incident while walking home. Why had George referred to me as his friend? He seemed to have been defending me from his father even as he vented his own frustration. I had always made it a point to avoid him and was less than flattered by this sudden esteem.

Rain began to fall and an unremarkable moon paid visits between passing clouds. I tilted my head toward the ground and scrunched my neck into the collar of my coat. Streetlights floated with wet newspaper in the puddles that gathered at the curbs of the sidewalks. At Saint Matthew's church, a man was urinating on bags of opened trash piled to a heap in the schoolyard beside it. He paused as I passed and for some reason I expected him to kill me. He seemed to have been excreted from the sewer. I thought of Emerson's complaint that if all the world was Philadelphia suicide would be extremely common, pleased to note the resumption of my normal, Alcestean ways.

The sight of someone looming in the opposite direction stalled me momentarily. His face was formless inside the shadows, but I had already identified him by his size and strut. I lowered my eyes, indented my shoulders and accelerated my pace. Hopefully, he wouldn't recognize me.

"Yo, cuz! Where-hare you goin' to?" I heard, three steps behind him.

His name was Hum, because it was. He'd been roaming the neighborhood since I was a child. He was anywhere between thirty and seventy-five. There was something obviously wrong with him, an enlarged heart, I believe, yet he was harmless. He knew and was known by everyone.

Hum was six feet ten inches at least, ascending like a lighthouse with a burnt-out bulb. The skin of his face stretched upward as if someone had pulled it from his cheeks to his ears in effort to crease a permanent smile, and his Adam's apple looked, oddly enough, like an apple lodged in his throat. If I didn't already know him, I would have run to the man from the sewer for help.

I looked up at him. "I'm going home," I said. "Why don't you?"

He gripped my head with his hand. "Home? But, hum, why, cuz?"

"Jesus, Hum, who let you out of the inferno?" I said, wriggling away. "Because it's late and it's raining, that's why."

"Yeah, hall-right! Li-histen to him! He said, hum, he said, ''Cause it's late!' and, hum, ''Cause it's raining!'"

"Goodbye."

"Yo, cuz, hold on!" He grabbed me.

"What?"

"Wait-hait hup a second!…I, hum, I seen your sis, cuz!"

"Did you? That's very nice."

"Ye-hep. She's hum, she's hum…very pretty!"

"I know."

"You-ha, you-ha mind if I, hum, I ask her out, too?"

"Go right ahead."

"Yeah, hall-right! Li-histen to him! He said, hum, he said, 'Go right ahead!'"

"Goodbye, Hum." I walked away. He followed.

"Yo, cuz!"

"*What?*"

"Wait-hait hup a second!…Why's hum, your si-hister, hum—"

"I don't know."

"But she's, hum, she-he's got, hum—"

"Look, Hum," I said, "I know why you're here, and you know why you're here, so you might as well just spit it out and get it over with…Whattaya need?"

"Hum?"

"Drugs, Hum! What drugs do you need? Quick, before the cops come."

"Hum?" he asked again, reeling. "I, hum…I don't do, hum…*Hum!*" he said, taking off in a goofy, ostrich-like jog down the street and out of sight. It was the only way to get rid of him, and never failed: he was frightened of cops and afraid of jail…as the saying goes.

Thus I continued on my solitary way, stopping once to let an empty bus rumble through a yellow light. Arriving at my street, I heard the strident sound of cats and caterwauling from the alleys behind the houses, sounding, I swear, like they were fucking each other to death. A perfect way to fall asleep, I thought, examining my keys in the dark before looking up and stopping short.

I moved closer, quietly, wanting for my initial impression to be proven false. It wasn't. Two shadows stood beneath the awning of my house. In my sister's arms, being caressed and consoled by her, was George Lestin.

He noticed me and extended his hand. "Hey, man, sorry 'bout that shit," he said.

I reacted impulsively, unconsciously…

As my sister screamed at me to stop, pulled my hair and scratched my face in his defense, I knew that she was lost to me, that I had lost her to him.

She was younger, then, and in love. She was finished.

Horatio Confused

For a long time there was nothing. Had he been conscious of it, he would have gloated. (Being correct, but unable to brag, is the atheist's tragedy). Both the tunnel and the supernatural light-at-the-end-of-it had been replaced by something neither white nor black, something absent even of the absence of light—which could only be described as nothing. It was like this for a very long time. Then, out of the formless void, from the face of the deep, a face appeared. It was his own, just as the body attached to it was himself. Behind him, a scene began to settle, slowly and brightly, from right to left, as if a curtain had been drawn upon a hidden Earth, which, gazing downward, he now could feel beneath his feet.

Gray-fingered dawn was threatening to break above a deserted street and its attendant houses, all of which were quiet, save for one. Its lights were on, its windows open, and people could be seen milling about at the base of its stairs. He sensed that there was someone in the house that he was waiting for, a friend of his…someone…Shock.

The screen door kicked open as he approached the porch. Shock ran out and past him, yanking him by the sleeve, yelling at him to "Come on!" Across the street, he recognized his car, parked sloppily and illegally in front of someone's garage. He unlocked the doors (*"Hurry up! Hurry up! Hurry up!"*), started the car and sped away.

"What the hell is your problem?" he asked, catching his breath.

"I'll tell you. Run this light first. Run it!"

He ran it.

"All hell was about to break loose in there," Shock said, equally winded. "Pandemonium. What a great word to call it."

"What did you do?"

Shock lit a cigarette. "You know that girl I was talking to?"

"Who, the blond?"

"Yeah, the blond…Fuckin' idiot. I beat the *shit* out of her."

"You *what*? Why?"

Shock shrugged. "She deserved it. What? She made me sick."

"What'd she do?"

"She's a fuckin' idiot! Don't get me wrong, I knew she was an idiot the moment I started talking to her. I just didn't know how *much* of an idiot. And what bothered me was, she didn't even *care* that she was an idiot. She was so content, so pig-in-shit satisfied with her own idiocy, I mean, *proud* of it. I couldn't take it anymore, so I smacked her."

"Where?"

"Where do you think?"

"Yeah, I know, I mean…How many times?"

"What? Did I smack her? I smacked the shit out of her, believe me."

He shook his head incredulously. "Are you insane?"

"What? You never wanted to smack someone for being stupid?"

"Yeah but you don't go fuckin' *do* it."

"Nah, that's the problem," Shock said, locking his hands behind his head. "If you wanna do it, then do it. Or else they get away with it."

"Did you warn her or anything? Or did you just hit her?"

"Well, yes and no. I mean, I didn't *tell* her I was gonna hit her, but I gave her a chance to get out of it. Actually, I gave her two chances. I asked her *two* questions. All she had to do was answer one of'em. Is it my fault she couldn't answer a simple fuckin' question?"

"What did you ask?"

"Listen how simple. I asked her, 'Who's the leader of the Nazis?' That's all."

"And she didn't know?" he laughed.

"No she didn't know! She told me Alfred Hitchcock!"

"No she didn't."

"I swear to God, she told me Alfred Hitchcock was the leader of the Nazis."

"I don't believe it."

"Why would I lie? Then I asked her to tell me who Sigmund Freud was."

"Now that's a little more difficult. She don't know who Hitler is, I'm guessin' she's ain't up to date on Freud."

Shock paused for effect. "You ready for this?"

"What, what she say?"

"She said (Shock imitated her voice), 'You mean them two fags?…With the lions?…One of'em almost ate the guy?'"

"Almost ate the guy…"

"Out in Vegas?"

"Vegas…You mean *Siegfried and Roy!*…No she didn't."

"Yes she did."

"No way. She did *not* say Siegfried and Roy!"

"Don't fuckin' laugh!" Shock yelled. "It isn't funny. It's pathetic."

"Well, yeah. But it's still pretty funny."

"No it isn't. It's insulting…You see why I had to smack her. Was practically begging me."

"How'd you do it?" he asked, still laughing. "Did you hit her as soon as she answered, or…?"

"Yeah, as soon as I figured out what she meant (I had to think), I reared back—*all* the way back (*that* was kinda funny)—and just *wailed* on her. Really. Like four or five times until somebody threw me off her (we were in the kitchen) and all hell broke loose. Then I ran outside and grabbed you. What were you doing out there, anyway?"

"I don't know…fresh air," he said. "What if I wasn't? You were gonna leave me in there?"

"It was life or death, man. You understand."

"Thanks a lot."

"No, don't be like that! They didn't even know we were together."

"You're right. How could they? I mean, all we did was show up together."

"C'mon! You woulda got out! They would have—Hold on," Shock grabbed his arm, "where you going?"

He didn't know. He'd been looking at Shock the entire time. Facing forward, he realized (or rather remembered) that he had also been driving, and, surveying the scene, that he was taking Shock home.

"I'm taking you home," he said.

"We can't go home *yet*," Shock said. "You wanna go *home*?"

Gray-fingered dawn, making good on its threat, had broken above the still-deserted streets and their attendant houses, whose cracked faces were now visible in the dull, gray morning.

"What else can we do?" he asked.

"I don't know. But we can't go home," Shock said, thinking. "Take me to my uncle's house."

"For what?"

"We'll get his gun."

He recalled his confusion then, just as it repeated itself now. "What do you want his gun for?"

"I don't know. We'll take it somewhere—Southern's schoolyard, or something—fuck around. Look at the stars," Shock pointed out of his window to the sky, "the lingering stars," he said, waxing poetic. "They should be punished for their loitering, don't ya think? Whattaya say, Joxer, we shoot'em out? We shoot out the stars?"

"I'm not firing a gun at the sky," he said. "Knowing my luck, the bullet'll fall to the earth and kill somebody. Let the stars stay if they wanna stay."

"We don't *have* to shoot *stars*. We can shoot other things. Line up some cans on a fence, I don't know."

"What are you, a fuckin' okie all of a sudden?...I want nothing to do with your uncle's gun."

"Fine," Shock said. "But we can't go home."

"Fine, then, we won't. Where would you like to go?"

The ensuing silence between them enabled him to recollect the series of events leading up to their great escape. The night began earlier than usual at the wedding serenade of a friend of a friend, due to be hitched on the following afternoon, which they had more or less crashed. Remembering this, he became aware of just how drunk he really was, how presumably drunk Shock must be. From the serenade, they proceeded to the house of a friend of a girl whom Shock had met while waiting in line for the bathroom, more or less to crash a party, which, as she informed him, would last "until morning." What followed was something of a controlled chaos of alcohol and drugs—controlled, that is, until Shock took umbrage with a "fuckin' idiot" and all hell broke loose.

"I got it," Shock said. "You ready?"

"What?"

"A.C."

"No," he shook his head, "No, I can't. Not tonight."

"Why not?"

"'Cause I got 20 dollars in my pocket."

"So what? I got 10."

"Then what's the point?"

"The point is, look at tonight. When it started, did you really think we'd end up at that girl's house? At that party? That Hitler would cause such a furor, pun intended? The point is, you never know. Let's keep it goin'. Like somebody said, there'll be enough time for sleeping when your dead."

"Somebody? Who?"

"I forget."

"That's a shame. It could have changed my mind."

"You see? That's your problem. Always pullin' out. Leave it in for once, Goddammit! So what she gets pregnant? She might not!"

"Interesting."

"Listen," Shock said. "We go to A.C., we put thirty on black, on red, I don't care—your call—and we either go home broke or we got sixty dollars to play around with. And who knows? It's A.C.! You know what that stands for, don't you?"

"What?"

"I can't think of anything right now. But it doesn't matter! You get the point!"

"Do you know what kind of people are at A.C. at 6 in the morning?"

"Us?"

"No. Hookers. And degenerates."

"Perfect, we'll fit right in."

"And on top of that," he said, "I shouldn't be driving."

"You shouldn't be sleeping, either…Excuse me a second. What's that? Hold on, I can't hear you." Shock put an imaginary phone to his ear. "What'd you say? We've hit a wall?…Yes, I believe you're right." Shock hung up and turned to him. "It seems to me you've been checkmated, my friend."

At the walls of his stomach, layers of dread began to peel, rolling all their strength and all their bitterness up into a ball, and though he could not say what it was he feared, he seemed at the same time to know exactly, as if he were somehow reliving the present, as if present and past had been yoked by violence together.

"All right, we'll go," he repeated, painfully.

Shock let out a yelp or a yawp or something of the kind. "I knew it! I knew you had heart! *Cor cordium*, that's you! Heart of hearts. Go ahead, try to burn it. You can't! Watch, I'll pluck it from the fire." Shocked plucked it from the fire. "What I tell ya? Not a blemish! See?"

"Yeah, but Trelawney lied," he said, sullenly, making a U-turn toward the Walt Whitman Bridge.

On the sidewalks of storefronts, life in moderation resumed. Stragglers scurried indoors, and old men felt safe enough to come out. In the sky, clouds were formed like distended faces of asphyxiated children. A sunless world spun through space unaccounted for.

"You're lucky you made it out of there alive tonight," he said, swerving to a stop at a light.

Shock, who was rummaging through his pockets, paused long enough to make a face.

"You can't go around slapping people."

"Here it is," Shock said, dangling a watch. "Time regained! Ha!" He fastened it around his wrist.

"I'm serious."

"About what? Really, what could they have done to me?"

"Let's see…"

"No no no. Let me rephrase the question. What could they have done to *me*? *To me*? Not you. To *me*."

"What's the difference?"

"The difference is, right now, I'm invulnerable. Didn't I tell you? Like Achilles, ankles and all into the River Styx. What name did Achilles assume among women? Go ahead, say it…Don't be scared."

"Shock?"

"That's right, Shock."

"As usual," he said, sighing, honking at a group of pigeons congregating over crumbs in the middle of the street, "your humility is endless."

"Humility is endless because weakness is everywhere and humility is for the weak."

"You've been practicing that, haven't you, Zarathustra?"

"Honestly, yes."

"And your invulnerability? When did this happen?"

"Didn't I tell you?"

"No."

"I thought I told you."

"Not that I remember."

"Are you sure? I could have sworn I told you. Or I've been meaning to tell you. Anyway," Shock cleared his throat, "I've come to the conclusion, or should I say, the conclusion came to me—that sounded like *Norwegian Wood*, didn't it?—that I am destined for greatness. How can this be, you ask? I can't say. But I sense it and I'm surprised by joy…You see what I did there? It's called a compound allusion."

"Truly you are marked for greatness."

"And not only that," Shock said without irony. "Here's where it gets interesting. The whole idea is, that a great man cannot die before his time, that he's invulnerable until his work is finished. His greatness protects him, keeps him safe, isn't at the mercy of catastrophe, asserts itself against the forces of chance, which obey it. And ever since, I've been tempting fate, throwing caution to the wind, so to speak. The more extreme the situation, the more dangerous it is, the better. Each time I escape, the more convinced I am. For instance, two nights ago, I had my uncle's gun—"

"Stop it, stop," he said, actually stopping. "I don't even wanna hear it."

"What?"

"What is wrong with you?"

"Nothing. I needed proof."

"By shooting yourself?"

"I'm here ain't I?"

He rolled his eyes. "Who *does* shit like this?"

"I told you. Right now, I'm invulnerable."

"You're lucky to be alive," he said, driving again. "Why do you have to take things so far? What was it last month? You were reading Hamsun and you decided to starve yourself because—what was it?—your physical state should rival your mental state, was that it? Or was it your spiritual state? I forget. Let me just say that judging by the way you ate tonight, I'd say you're over it. A hunger artist you're not."

"No, but it's funny you should bring that up," Shock said, patiently. "Because Knut is a great example. He gets tuberculosis, and what does he do? Rides on top of a train from Minnesota to New York with his mouth open until the cold air cures him. See? He hadn't yet written the books he'd be remembered for. Therefore, not even tuberculosis could harm him. He was *invulnerable*. And the sheer audacity to ride atop a train for three days, or however long it was back then, and arrive safely—he knew he was great, that there was nothing for him to fear."

"Hamsun supported Hitchcock," he said, making the long left onto Broad Street.

"Ah, but time that with this strange excuse will pardon Kipling and his views," Shock smiled, leaning his head out of the window to inform an old man at a newsstand of the fate of Paul Claudel. The old man waved in agreement.

"Sounds to me like another one of your theories du jour," he said when Shock returned to his seat, "I think you've been reading too much Carlyle. Didn't Tolstoy expose Napoleon as a fraud? Not to mention the fact that the poor bastard thought Odin was an actual person. Too much ice water in the morning, can't be good."

"I prefer *Representative Men*," Shock said.

"Swedenborg?"

"Besides Swedenborg."

"Why? I especially liked his *The Pleasures of Insanity Concerning Your Sister's Ass*…Which reminds me that I, too, have a theory: that all of these self-proclaimed prophets, at least those who last, like Swedenborg, were schizophrenic, only they had the good fortune of being geniuses too. Lots of schizophrenics think they're prophets, but they aren't geniuses too, which means they can't write the books that make them famous, or convince disciples to follow them around. And Jesus Christ was quite simply both a schizophrenic and a genius, the first to fancy himself not only a prophet, but the son of God—that was his great, sick, blasphemous innovation, and because of his genius he pulled it off. And we've been paying for it ever since."

"He wasn't the first," Shock huffed.

"No? Then who was?"

"Never mind. And stop changing the subject! As for Tolstoy—who was it said it?—that he thought he was God's older brother? He wrote just to hear himself read. Napoleon's army invaded his country, and French invaded his books. Bitterness is all. And before I forget," Shock burped, "there's much to be said about Carlyle, because History *is* the story of great men, and greatness *is* a universal element, *the* universal element. It should have a symbol on the periodic table."

"I don't know about that," he said. "I'm more inclined to think stupidity, if anything, was the uncaused cause, the prime mover. In fact, I'm beginning to think it's stupidity that controls the weather. Like, for instance, you hear of earthquakes—is an earthquake considered weather?—in Turkey, for instance, or, I don't know, mudslides in Mexico—too much stupidity concentrated in one place at one time—the atmosphere can't handle it. Which is probably why at that party tonight I was standing outside. Too many stupid people. I was afraid the ceiling was gonna collapse. Or like at weddings or funerals, wherever two or three are gathered in His name, I find the nearest exit and stand there. I'm tellin' you, it's bound to happen. Something just explodes. Do you remember when—"

"Are you done?" Shock interrupted.

"Yeah, I'm just—"

"Because that's exactly the kind of thing that separates us."

"What is?"

"Thinking stupidity has a place higher than greatness in the order of things. Just because it's more prevalent doesn't mean it's more dominant, does it? You asked me, 'What's the difference?' *That's* the difference between me and you."

"And let me guess, another example why you're 'invulnerable' and I'm not."

"You said it."

To their right, Marconi Park was desolate save for the homeless asleep on its benches and the statue of Columbus leaning upon the Earth he was about to map with syphilis.

"How 'bout this then?" he said, acknowledging the arrival of the anger he'd been expecting, which, nonetheless, took him by surprise. "Suppose we crash? What happens then? You survive, I end up brain dead? Is that how it works? Because, I mean, you're great and everything, right?"

Shock massaged his temples with his thumb and middle finger as if coaxing the thoughts from his head. "I didn't say you'd die," he said. "All I said is that great men cannot die before their time. So if we crash, yeah, I suppose I'd survive. I'm not saying you *wouldn't*, but I know I would. Let me give you another example. Byron—he did what Leander couldn't do—"

"Leander *did* do it. He fucked up once."

"You know what I mean. Byron wasn't overtaken by storms, was he? No, because his work had yet to be finished. If he'd fought for the Greeks at 25, he would have survived. If he tried to swim the Hellespont after completing his thirty-sixth year, who knows? Chances are he would have drowned."

"And what about Chatterton?" he said. "All that potential, dead?"

"If that were the case, his suicide would have failed. Because it was successful, we can safely say, Chatterton was a failure. Look at Keats. You think he could have made his awkward bow before finishing the Odes? Of course not. Keats is Chatterton realized."

"Let me remind you that Chatterton did more at 12 than you've done yet."

"Let *me* remind *you* that Cervantes needed until he was 60 to write *Don Quixote*. There's no such thing as a timetable. His greatness kept him alive through slavery and imprisonment."

At the end of a semi-circular ramp, negotiated with only a modicum of difficulty, the unspectacular framework of the Walt Whitman Bridge appeared, so named in honor of the poet's decision to have a stroke while visiting his mother in Camden, leaving him partially paralyzed and stranding him there for the final 19 years of his life.

"Let me just say how happy I am to know all this," he said, merging. "I feel infinitely more secure in your presence, not to mention, insignificant."

Shock put his hand on his shoulder, "Don't take it too hard," he said in a tone suggesting wisdom retained from a past life. "Some men are born to be Braque, others Picasso. There's no shame in it. I happen to like Braque. So what he hitched his wagon to a star? It happens all the time. Some men are born to be Boswells, others Johnsons; some Engles, some Marx."

"Don't forget Kafka and Goethe," he said, having heard it all before, only never directed at himself.

"Exactly. Max Brod to Kafka, Eckermann to Goethe, and, speaking fictitiously, of course, Horatio to Hamlet."

"I see, so I'm Horatio now?"

"Time will tell," Shock shrugged. "Just do me this favor, no matter what I say to you, no matter how much I plead, do *not* toss my manuscripts into the fire. And please, could you remember, please, to report me and my cause aright to the unsatisfied?"

"Don't believe it," he said, accelerating. "And while we're at it, let me be the first to tell you that I think your 'great men never die' theory is total bullshit and I'm embarrassed for you. I'd like to see you take a running fuckin' jump off of Liberty 1 and see what happens—or would a host of angels rush to your rescue?"

Shock laughed and spoke calmly, "Of course not *angels*. But *something* would happen. Something would prevent me from taking a running fuckin' jump."

"You really believe that, don't you?"

"It's not my fault if you don't believe me. Maybe you resent that you can't sense it yourself. I feel it and I know it's true."

"So the angels, they don't catch you, they just, what, block your path?"

"Who said anything about angels? I simply said that *something* would stop me. Like Dostoevsky. The last second reprieve in front of the firing squad. Something like that."

"Oh, I get it. The *Tsar* is going to save you. That makes sense."

"You can laugh all you want," Shock said. "But right now, at this moment, nothing frightens me. Right now, for me at least, death doesn't exist. Maybe *you'd* be undone by it, not me. You want proof? I'll give you proof if you want it. I'm serious. Just say the word." Shock awaited the word in a prolonged silence between them.

"I'll tell you what I do want," he said at last. "Toll money. Okay, Prince of Fuckin' Danes? Save some of that ten dollars for the ride home. I'm sick of paying your way. You're real good at fallin' asleep the moment they're in sight. My uncle has a name for people like you: Nicky No-tolls he'd call you."

Shock turned in his seat and stared at him. "Here," he said, throwing a balled up ten dollar bill on the dashboard.

"I said for the ride home. I don't want it now."

"Well you better take it now, or you won't be getting it at all."

"I'm used to it, believe me."

"I had a feeling this would happen."

"What?"

"That I'd have to prove it to you."

"Prove what? You're great? I believe you. Now will you give it a rest?"

"How can great men be great unless they're believed in?"

"Jesus Christ, didn't you just hear me say I believed you?"

"I'll prove it to you."

"I don't want you to prove it."

"Now I have to."

"No, really, you don't."

Shock removed his watch. "Here," he said, handing it to him

"What's this for?"

"Keep it safe. I want it back."

That being said, Shock calmly and without hesitation unlocked the passenger side door and jumped, just like that, out of a moving car on the Walt Whitman Bridge. Flights of angels did not impede his rest...

As he yanked the wheel in an instinctive effort to stop his friend, his car slammed once again into the concrete barrier separating the highway from the bridge's green, steel beams. And as his car slammed once again into this barrier, he awoke and for a long time remembered nothing.

A Spur Moment

It has long been proven that when we alive awaken the dead of night will be as dead, which is why, since the sweeping up the heart is solemn work, I prefer to get a good night's sleep before the bedlam breaks and refuse to answer telephone or doorbell past a certain hour. It is better not to know for whom it tolls. If it happens to be a friend in need—and when are they your friends if not in need?—well, then, he should have known his needs at a more reasonable hour. If it happens to be otherwise, especially at your door, well, then, more than likely it tolls for thee; it is a truth universally acknowledged that a single man in possession of even a modest fortune must be wary of his life.

Thus, when my doorbell buzzed at 4:22 a.m., I knew it to be more trouble than it was worth (alas, our need to learn that which we already know is the essence of human nature). Normally, I would lie motionless, eyes closed, breath held, waiting for whomever it was to give up and go home. But on this particular night, I was drunk enough to be brave, bored enough to be curious, and, against my better judgment, I answered the goddamned door.

It was a friend of mine (though not a close friend, and certainly not close enough to warrant so late a visit), and a girl I had never met. I wanted to start over. He looked as if his night had started, say, four or five nights ago. She looked, to be kind, sloppy.

He was finishing a phone call and instructed me with one finger to "wait a minute."

"Yeah. Yeah. Yeah? Uh-huh. Yeah. No. I gotta go. Yeah. Later." He shook my hand. "Yo, John! What's goin' on? This is—what's your name?"

"Melissa."

"Melissa. Melissa, this is John."

"Hi, John."

"Hello."

"You think we could come up real quick?"

"Why, what's wrong?"

"Nothing. Let us in."

I led them upstairs, sulking.

"Can I use your bathroom?" Melissa asked.

"Sure. It's over there." She followed my finger. I hoped that was all.

"So how you doin', John? Haven't seen you for a while."

"Good, Stein (his name)," I said. "And you? You look like you had a rough night."

"Me? Nah! This is only the beginning!"

Oh no.

It was necessary to handle Stein in small doses. It took practice. I was introduced to him as a kid, when he was expelled from his elementary school and transferred to mine. He appeared before the class wearing horn-rim glasses, which, as kids do, we considered a sign of abnormal intelligence, and which, as kids will, we ridiculed before given proof. Never before had a nickname been less compatible with what inspired it. Stein was a nice enough guy, it was just, he tended to be, well, crooked and criminal...But nice.

His world and mine didn't often intersect, and I apologize in advance for his crudity. He was one of those people for whom the concept of consequence was like calculus. "Because," from what I had gathered, was the centerpiece of his philosophy. He was still tinkering with it at the time; God help us all if he ever perfected it. I once heard a story that his parents took a cruise to Bermuda and commissioned Stein's godmother to live with him in their house while they were gone. They expected their son, if left own his own, would blow the whole street sky-high. He was twenty-five years old, by the way. And so what if he had shown up on my doorstep at 4:22 a.m.? What a devil had he to do with the time of the day?

Stein pulled my ear to his mouth and spoke softly. I had the strange feeling that I was becoming a partner in crime.

"Can we use your back room?" he asked. "Not for long. Just a little." He whistled and pumped the air twice with his fist. "We got nowhere else to go. You know how it is."

I didn't. "You can't be serious," I said.

"What?"

"You came here to get *laid*?"

"Why? You wanna come back there with us?" He looked both ways cautiously as if crossing the street with a child and putting his hand on my shoulder said, "She's like that." His eyebrows arched.

"No thanks, Stein. Just be quick."

"In and out, John."

"I mean it."

"In and out, I swear."

It was pointless to argue; he had crossed the threshold. I had invited him to my apartment once before, months ago, and he had kept me up until breakfast, which, incidentally, he insisted I pay for. He must have noticed the spare bed in the back room and carried its memory like an ace in the hole for just this sort of crisis. You had to admire his foresight.

"Last night, John, listen to this," he said, bouncing back and forth on his heels. "I was with this girl, right? She was sittin' across the bar with her friends. I told her, 'com'ere,' like this, you know? (He demonstrated with his index finger.) And at first she didn't see me. But then she was like, 'Me?' I said, 'Yeah, you!' So she comes, right? And she's like, 'Whattaya want?" I told her, 'I bet that's the first time a guy made you come with one finger! You get it? Come with one finger?"

"I got it," I said.

"Took her to Ferrlo's house…Gave it to her…Wait, there was somethin' else…Oh yeah! You know there's a new whorehouse opened up? Two doors down?"

"From who?"

"From you!"

"Me?"

"Yeah! Two strippers. They got a three-year-old up there. I was up there smokin' with'em."

"With who the three-year-old?"

"No! The strippers."

"When?"

"Last week…I rang your bell. You didn't answer."

"What time?"

"I don't know, late."

"Are you a customer of theirs?"

"Who me? Please. You know I don't pay for it, John."

"That's right. How could I forget?"

"You know what I mean?" He knocked on the bathroom door. "What's she doin' in there?" He knocked again. "Hurry it up, sweetie!" No reply. He listened for a while then lit a cigarette.

"Mind if I smoke?"

"No."

"She was gonna squat. I told her hold it in."

"Stein, I'm serious," I said. "You gotta be fast back there."

"John, I ain't gonna *kiss* her!"

The bathroom door opened. What's-Her-Name came out and stood at attention.

"It's about time!" Stein shouted. "You hear me knockin'?"

"No," she said, quickly, looking around.

"You on the rag or somethin'? Don't tell me you're on the rag."

She shook her head, "no."

"Better not be," Stein said, pushing her through the kitchen and into the back room. The door slammed. I cursed creatively.

I was suddenly sober and tired. I needed something to do. I poked around in an ashtray for a roach, found one, smoked it and tried to stay awake. The girl had probably cased the place at first sight. She wasn't, again, being kind, the most polished debutante at the ball. I raised the volume to the infomercial on the television. *New non-stick pots and pans!* Housewives gasped. As it turned out, Stein's beloved was a screamer. Whatever they were doing, it sounded closer to birth than conception.

I had begun to doze, or maybe I was sound asleep, when Valmont returned. He was standing over me, staring.

"How long you been out here?" I asked, stretching.

"Not long. Why? You nervous?"

"No…I'm just wondering."

"Couple minutes." He looked at his watch.

"What time is it?"

"6:33."

"6:33! What the fuck happened to 'in and out'?"

"I tried, John. You know me." He smiled.

"Where's the girl?" I asked.

"Huh?"

"The girl…Where is she?"

"Oh! She's sleepin'."

"Why don't you wake her? I'm going to bed."

"Going to bed! It's Friday night!"

"It is to you."

"Let her sleep," he waved his arm. "Hang out for a while…We'll smoke."

Stein had discovered what I had foolishly stashed in a coffee cup on a windowsill and invited himself. This, I could tell, would continue until he made me pay for breakfast. He unrolled the plastic bag, broke the seal, and sniffed inside like a connoisseur. "It'll do," he said. He pulled papers, a pipe, a phone, and a bag of coke from the pockets of his Phillies jacket, and a gun from a holster fastened to the back of his belt. He stacked the items on the table in front of him and began to segregate the stems and seeds. I thought of something to say besides the obvious.

"Doesn't your sister work at that bank on 15th street?" I said.

"Uh-huh."

"I thought I saw her. She must have been on break or something. I saw her outside smoking."

"Smoking what? A cigarette? I'll kill her!" Stein packed a bowl, lit it and inhaled. He repeated and offered it to me. I waved him off.

"What were you doin' over there?" he asked and exhaled.

"Where?"

"My sister's bank?"

"What I always do."

"That's where you go?"

"Yeah…Why?"

"Nothin'." He inhaled again. "You know if they're open on Saturdays?"

"Yeah…Why?"

"Nothin'." He exhaled again.

I changed the subject. "Where'd you meet that girl?" I said, watching the slow swirl of smoke circle momentarily above his head before meeting its fate in the ceiling fan.

"What girl?"

"The girl you came with?"

"Oh! At the gas station. Round your corner. She asked if I had anything." He wiggled the coke. "I told her, 'First line's on me…Where do you want it?' You get it? First line's *on me*?"

"So you took her to my apartment? That's where she wanted it?"

"Hey, I thought I was doin' you a favor!" He tapped his pipe on the side of an ashtray. "Too late now."

"What else did you give her?" I said.

"Whattaya mean?"

"Most people don't sleep on that stuff."

"What stuff?" He lit a cigarette. "The coke? She never even got to do it! I put her right to sleep. I told you I don't pay for it, John."

"That's right..." I gave the most animated yawn followed by the most conspicuous sigh of my life.

"What's wrong with you?" he asked. "You wanna eat or somethin'? Watch a movie?"

"No, I wanna go to bed."

"Go to bed!"

"Yes, Stein, that's what people do at 6 in the morning. They go to bed. You and your girl are gonna have to leave...I'm sorry."

"Don't be sorry, John...It ain't your fault. We'll do a line. That'll wake you up." He grabbed a deck of cards from the top of the television, then searched the floor and picked up the *Collected Shakespeare* at my feet. It suddenly occurred to me what a wonderful weapon it would make. Forsooth, I could bash his brains in.

"Shakespeare!" he said. "To be drunk or not, right? Ain't that the question?" He bellied over.

"Burbage himself couldn't do it better," I said.

"Who?"

"No one. But I am glad to hear you know Hamlet."

He stopped laughing. "Hamlin? Who, from Two Street?"

"Uh, no, from Denmark."

"Denmark?" He shook his head. "Never heard of him. I only know the one from Two Street. You know him?"

"Nope."

"Yes you do! He had the father, murdered by the uncle? Girlfriend went crazy, killed herself? Why, what he do now?"

"What did who do now?"

"Hamlin?"

"I just told you I have no idea who you're talking about."

"You brought him up," he said.

I cracked my knuckles. "Here's one," I said. "Why is it that Leopold Bloom never cracks his knuckles? Answer that. I mean, he does everything else."

Stein thought about it. "I don't know."

"Neither do I...I mean, he takes a shit, he jerks off...Wait a minute, did you say his *father* was murdered by his *uncle*?"

"Who, Hamlin? Yeah. The uncle was fuckin' the mom. He married her and everything."

"I can't believe it," I said.

"What?"

"Nothing…Never mind."

Atlas shrugged and spread the cards across the coffee table. "Gotta use the king of clubs, John," he said. "Remember that. Always use the king of clubs." He chopped two thick lines on Shakespeare's face.

"Now why you gonna do that?" I protested.

"What?"

"Using Shakespeare for that?"

"Why?"

"Because it's Shakespeare. It's disrespectful."

"No it's not. What about the Bible? When you roll a joint with the pages?"

"That's different."

"Why?"

"Because it's Shakespeare!"

"So what? He did 'em too! Him and…What's-His-Face?"

"Who?"

"I don't know. That guy. You want one or not?"

"No."

"I thought you said you wanted one?"

"I never said I wanted one."

"What is *wrong* with you?" He rolled a dollar bill and did them both. "Smells so good," he said as the *Ode to Joy* began to play. Stein answered his phone.

"Hell-o. Yeah. I'm at Johnny's. Nah, Grantini's. You know him! He lives on Shunk Street. Trust me, you know him. Short guy? Goin' bald?"

I winced.

"Nothin'. We're smokin'. Just did a rope. Huh? No, I brought some girl over. Yeah. Gave it to her. He didn't want it. I don't know, I asked him. Yeah. Back-door. I'll tell you later. Nothin'! I'll tell you later! Yeah. At the gas station. Listen to this! We get in the bedroom, right? And she's like, 'Ew, you smell good. Whattaya got on?' And I'm like, 'A hard-on, sweetie, but I didn't think you could smell it!'"

I admit I laughed.

"Where yous at? Did yous? Yeah. I know. I'll call you later. Who is? She *what*? You told her she's got a mouth and an asshole, right? Yeah. Yeah. Yeah. Yeah? Yeah. Later." He hung up.

"That was Ferrlo...Said hello."

"Did he? That's nice...Who's Ferrlo?"

"Ferrlo! You know him! Used to put the meat in the shoebox? 'Member? Had the hole and the hair? Used to...you know!"

"Ugh..." I cringed. "That was *him*? He's still alive?"

"Yeah, he's alive! He's over Scarole's house."

"*Bobby* Scarole?...Isn't he dead?"

"No, he ain't dead!"

"I heard he got shot."

"He did! Him and his two brothers, over around Snyder Avenue."

"And they didn't die?"

"No!"

"Are you sure?"

"I just talked to them yesterday," Stein said impatiently.

"Then who shot them?"

"I'on't know," he hummed.

"The Brothers Scarole," I said. "I remember them when they were kids. Dostoevsky woulda had a field day with them."

"Listen," Stein said, wagging his finger. "I been thinkin'. That girl's gotta stay...She'll wake up tomorrow, won't remember where she is and forget all about me...That's the way I like it."

"You're crazy, right?" I said, stretching again.

"Whattaya mean, 'crazy'? Why not? She wakes up, and you get it in the mornin'. What's wrong with that?"

"What's wrong with that! *You're* the one who brought her here. She's your problem."

"She's nobody's problem, John, believe me."

"I'm not keeping some girl you picked up at a gas station just because, 'that's the way you like it'? No way." My head was spinning.

"C'mon, John. I'll owe you one," he said.

"I don't want her here! She'll probably rob me blind!"

"Don't worry about *that*."

"I'm waking her," I said, heading toward the bedroom.

"John, wait! Hold up. John!" He trailed after me, hooking my shirtsleeve with his hand. "I'll get her. Just hold on. Sit down. Why you wanna blow my cover?"

"What cover?"

"She knows my girlfriend," he said, leading me back to the living room. "I didn't know at the time."

"Whose fault is that, Stein?"

"It's nobody's fault, John. Just enjoy yourself. Get a beer. You got any beer?"

"In the refrigerator."

He went to the kitchen and came back with two cans. "You ever do a rip cord?" he asked.

"What? No. Just drink," I said.

"Really, you never did one?"

"No. In high school."

"Watch." He took a key, punctured the bottom of the can, put his mouth to the hole, opened the beer and drained it, but not without dripping half of it down his chin and on his shirt. He wiped his mouth with his sleeve.

"Cords are the best," he said. "You get more drunker. Me and Little Rocky—You know Little Rocky, don't you? Kid with the brain tumor?"

I nodded.

"We were doin' cords down the shore one time, right? And we do, like, I don't know, a whole case in like a half hour and go to the boardwalk, right? John...Soon as we get there, Rocky passes out in front of the tramcar. Right in front of the fuckin' tramcar, flat on his face. And the driver's all pissed off, yellin' and screamin', honkin' at him, '*Watch the tramcar please. Watch, watch, watch, the tram car please!*' John, I swear, for like ten minutes! It was the *fuckin' best*! We had to carry him home."

"From the shore?"

"No! To the motel. You shoulda seen it. We got back to the room and shaved his head."

"Didn't that aggravate the tumor?"

"Nah, that was later...But that weekend, right, Brownie's comin' down to meet us, right, and these cops, they pull him over. 'Member Brownie? Stole the fence around Johnson's field? Sold the aluminum?...You 'member?"

I nodded.

"I remember one time, right, he stole his cousin's bike she got for Holy Communion. Sold it 'round the corner for eleven dollars."

"Nice guy."

"Yeah. They don't let him go to family parties no more."

"I wonder why."

"'Cause of the bike."

"I know, Stein, 'cause of the bike…So what happened?"

"When?"

"When the cops pulled him—forget it." I yawned again.

"What's a matter?"

"Nothing, Stein. I'm tired."

"*Still?*"

"Yes."

He looked around my apartment. "I don't know what else we could do," he said. "You got any vodka?"

"No."

"No? Damn. I coulda showed you somethin'. You ever snorted it?"

"I think you've snorted enough," I said.

"Why, you never snorted it? Aw, it's the *fuckin' best*! You get one of them rock glasses, right? Turn it upside down and fill in that caved-in part—you know, that caved in part?—with vodka. Then you snort it."

"Can't you just drink it?"

"You get more drunker."

I put my head in my hands.

"What about power hours?" I heard him ask. "Y'ever do a power hour?"

"It's 7 o'clock in the morning!"

"Yeeaaahh? And it'll be over by eight. What's the big deal?" He grabbed the remote from the table and started flicking. "You sure you ain't got no movies? No food?"

I had enough. "Stein, are you staying or not? 'Cause you're driving me crazy. There's a couch here if you wanna crash. Pull it out. I'm going to bed…Just, whenever you do leave, take that girl with you."

"Now John," he said, calmly, "I thought we agreed about the girl. If you want *me* to leave, that's fine. But the girl's gotta stay." He claimed my unopened beer, and, to his credit, drank it like a human being. A few gulps later, he said, "Lemme ask you somethin'."

Here it comes, I thought.

"I'll tell you why I came tonight…Why I *really* came."

"To get laid. I know. We've established that."

"No, besides that. I was comin' here anyway. That was was, like, a spur moment…I gave you a chance, though, didn't I?"

"You were very considerate."

"You know me, John! Comes around, goes around." He slapped my hand. "The things is, I got a problem…A little one. I need your help."

"Let me guess."

"What?"

"How much?"

He smiled. "You'll get it back, John. I promise…I got nowhere else to go."

"Again?"

"Whatta you mean?"

"You said that earlier."

"It's true! I tried callin' you yest—"

"Stein!"

"What?"

"Just tell me how much."

"Five."

"Hundred, I hope?"

"I wish, John. Thousand."

I opened the blinds. "See that, Stein? It's called the sun. It means it's time to go home."

He shielded his eyes. "Whattaya mean?" he said.

"I *mean*, it's time to go home."

"You're ain't even gonna think about it?"

"No, I thought about it. And I'm not giving you five thousand dollars."

"Why not? I know you got it!"

"That's not the point!" I shouted. "Just because I got it doesn't mean I'm gonna give it away!"

"You're not *givin'* it away, John…It's a loan."

"Sure it is."

"Look," he said. "I owe *Pigs*! You know Pigs? He gave me a week last Saturday. Guess what happens if I don't give him his money?"

"You shoulda thought of that first," I said.

"Thoughta what? Gettin' shot?…That's real nice, John. That's real nice to say to a friend."

"What do you want me to say, Stein? You're the one with the gun, use it."

We both looked.

"I'll give you one," I blurted out.

"You'll give me one?"

"Yes, one. To get rid of you."

"But before it was nothin'."

"Right. But I changed my mind."

"Why?"

"Because I did. Now do you want it or not?"

"No, I don't want it. I want five."

"I don't *have* five."

"That's too bad, John."

"If I don't have it, how the fuck am I supposed to give it to you!"

"That's the same thing I say to Pigs, but Pigs don't care." He chopped another line, snorted it like vodka and lit a cigarette. "I'll ask you again," he said. "One?...That's all you're gonna give me?"

"That's all I *got*."

He bit his lip and thought about it. "Nah," he shook his head, "can't do it."

"Well then I'm sorry, Stein."

"*You're* sorry?" He picked up his gun and unloaded it.

"What are you doing?" I asked.

"Look at these." He showed me a palm full of bullets. "These are cop killers. Uh-huh. Hollow tips. Go through vests." He rubbed his nose like he was trying to flatten it, reloaded the gun and put it on his lap. "You understand?" he asked.

"Do I understand what?"

He stood and pointed it at me. "I need five thousand dollars, John."

"Stein, this is insane. Will you fuckin' lower that!"

"I'm bein' serious, John. *Pigs* is insane."

"Let me get this straight, you come to my apartment, you fuck first, then you rob me at gun point? Is that it?"

"Relax, John. I offered her. You didn't want it...And I'm still gonna give you your money back."

"What about Ferrlo?"

"What about him?"

"Did you ask him?"

"Ferrlo!...Everybody knows he's broke!"

I took a quick glance at Shakespeare's powdered beard. Verily, he could do nothing for me now.

"Why don't you go home, Stein, get some sleep? We can talk about it tomorrow."

"John, are you that fuckin' stupid? I ain't *got* until tomorrow. It's already fuckin' tomorrow. You see that?" He pointed at the window. "That's called the sun."

"What am I supposed to do, Stein? I don't have five thousand dollars here! What do you think, I hide it under my mattress? It's in the fuckin' bank! You know, the bank? Where your sister works?"

"I'll take a check," he said, and was serious.

"Oh, will you? How convenient! Should I make it out to Carlo Piggliacci? Save you the trouble?"

"Nonono!" he said. "To me."

I stood motionless, closing my eyes and holding my breath, waiting for him to give up and go home.

"John?"…"John!"

"What?"

"What are you waitin' for? You want me to fire in the air or somethin'? He drew the hammer back. His hands were shaking, and his eyes were blinking wildly. He's aiming at me through a strobe light, I thought, and gave up. I wrote a check.

"Here," I said, handing it to him, "Just think, one of these days you might even earn one of these."

"What's that supposed to mean?"

"It means get a fuckin' job!"

"I got a job! I wash cars."

"Good for you. Now will you lower that fuckin' gun!"

He folded the check and gathered his things. "Thanks, John. Trust me, you'll see your money. I promise." He stopped by the stairs. "And that other thing. I'm sorry…I didn't know what else to do with it."

"Just get out. Please."

I heard the door behind him. And with that, ladies and gentlemen, we had reached the dregs. I sat down, stared stupidly at the television, and watched what had transpired replay in my head. "I'll take a check," he said. He'll take a check! I went to the bathroom. Coke was scattered across the *American Standard* stamp on the toilet tank. I blew it off and exited to the living room, mourning the loss of my money. What could I do? Call the police? On *Stein*? I fell asleep.

When I awoke in the afternoon, the events rushed over me anew and I remembered—what was it?—Melissa. I checked to see if anything was missing. No. I went to the back room, hoping she had already left. No. There she was in all her glory, still naked, and sleeping on her stomach. From the side, she looked younger than I remembered. I pushed and pulled at her.

"Let's go! Get up!…Hey! Sleeping beauty!" I clapped my hands. She didn't move. I rolled her over. She wouldn't wake. On the pillow beside her, a note had been placed. One word, scribbled hastily: *Accidint.*

Ah Sun-flower

Stephen stuffed himself deeper into the small space between the bed and the wall, the safest space between himself and Jane, who was smoking at the edge of the bed. Her legs crossed casually as she spun the ash forward and back along the inside of a silver ashtray. Stephen heard her sigh and sensed her eyes sliding furtively to their corners to gaze repeatedly at the back of his head. He thought of her eyes, and how the black overflowed into and consumed the white until it became their only color. It reminded him of the eyes in a portrait by Modigliani. Their unusual size caused her slender face to look by comparison as though it had preserved the aspect of its infancy. Stephen wrote of this quality to her in a series of anti-Petrarchan poems she appreciated without understanding. Apparently, he described the act to Jane as poorly as he performed it with her.

"Believe me, I understand," Jane counseled him, exhaling. "And I'm glad you told me. So enough with the embarrassment, okay? It's nothin' to be ashamed of." Except Stephen had cried during his confession and thought otherwise.

Stephen had come to Jane for his unsentimental education, though had kept this motive ulterior. He desired a Dark Lady to send him off in search of his Capulet. Little progress had been made thus far. The two of them had muddled through several unsatisfactory attempts, each lengthening the fall from the vertiginous heights he had presumed, and ending with Stephen hiding his face in the wallpaper. Jane, though patient throughout, had interrogated him tonight until he cracked. She had accidentally laughed when he revealed his reason and been apologizing for the past half-hour, relieved that it had nothing to do with her and everything to do with him. She liked Stephen, he was sensitive and smart, and, because of this, she was willing to work through any awkwardness. Who knew where it might lead?

"You understand, then?" Stephen said, coming to life on his back, squinting into the ceiling light to keep from looking at her.

Jane took a final drag and put her cigarette out. "Yeah, *now* I do," she said. "But I was beginning to get insulted. I thought you thought I was ugly. And I know I'm not *that* bad. It was just…very confusing."

"And you don't think any less of me?"

She snapped her tongue at him. "Don't be silly. I was the same way my first time. It's normal," she said, uncrossing her legs and putting the ashtray on the floor. "You did have me a little nervous, though. I thought you were gonna tell me you were gay or something. You *do* have that tattoo and all."

Stephen frowned. "I already told you about that."

"I know, but still."

Three years ago, or thereabout, Jane and a young man named Robert were eating lunch at the Penrose Diner. They had a booth by the window. It was their day at last. Robert had given her an ultimatum.

The two had met at a surprise party thrown for Robert's cousin. Jane had noticed him immediately. He came late and she thought he was the stripper her friends had hired as a prank. She never told him that. When she saw him shake hands with a group of guys at the bar, she realized her mistake. Much later, she asked the birthday girl to point her out and to tell him of her interest. This was a bold, uncharacteristic move on Jane's part, but since she had recently lost some weight, had quite a bit to drink, and was wearing one of the few outfits she owned that didn't entirely disgust her by the way it fit, she took her chances. Robert followed his cousin's pointed finger and liked what was attached to the other end of it: Jane, nearly melting, digging through her pocketbook. They did a few shots together and he teased her about the faces she made. They small-talked about themselves in general terms. He was a freshman at Philadelphia's Community College. He had taken a year off between High School to help out at his father's garage. She was a senior at Our Lady of Fatima High School for Girls and hadn't yet decided what she planned to do after graduation. "I'm not sure what I'm good at yet," she said. Their night ended with a hug and an exchange of phone numbers.

They spent the subsequent nights watching movies and drinking in Robert's apartment. Jane would only go so far before pulling back and removing his hands. She told him that she had just got out of a bad relationship and wanted to go slowly. She improvised a history of abuses committed by her former flame. Robert understood, and, to indicate this, ceased kissing her all together.

His phone calls became less frequent and eventually disappeared. She left messages that were never returned.

Jane had written him off and was heartbroken when he showed up at her door. He said that he couldn't stop thinking about her, that he wanted to be serious, that they should either, well, *be together*, or call it off. He was standing at her bottom step in a drizzling rain, reminding Jane of a closing scene to a romantic movie. She had become too attached, too soon, and fearing a second stalemate, she agreed.

They bought beer and walked to a nearby park. Jane ran to a swing and kicked it into motion. Robert caught up with her, grabbed the chains and stopped her momentum. He straddled her legs, began kissing her and unbuttoning her shirt. "What are you doing?" she said. "Not *here!*" "But you just said—" "I didn't mean right now!" "Then when?" "I don't know! Tomorrow night, I guess." "I won't be around tomorrow night." "Then earlier. In the afternoon," she said, pushing him away. "Don't lie to me," he said. "I'm not." And here they were.

"What's wrong?" Robert said. "You look nervous."

Jane finished chewing. "Should I be?"

"No. But you still look it. Tell me something. Was it really that bad?"

"Was what bad?"

"The last guy you were with."

"Who?…Oh! Him! Not really. I mean, he was nice—"

"*Nice*? Are we talkin' about the same guy?"

Jane scratched her face. "I lied," she said. "I'm sorry."

"About what?"

"About the whole 'bad relationship' thing. I never even *had* a relationship. I was just so surprised you even liked me. I don't know. That's never happened to me, and…I've never done it," she whispered. "But I want to, I do. I'm just scared, I guess."

"So you lied to me?" Robert said.

"Yeah, at first, but…I'm sorry!" Jane reached for his hand.

Robert leaned back in his seat. "You've never done it before?"

"No."

"You're a virgin?"

"That's how it works. Why, is it a problem?"

He looked distracted. "No, no, not at all," he said. "Wait, so, all along, *that* was your problem?"

"You just said it wasn't a problem!"

"No, I mean, *that's* why you've been acting that way?"

"I guess. It's just…I imagined you with all this experience, and me…I don't know. It's like, I'm afraid I won't know how and that I'll let you down, ya know?"

"We'll fix that, Jane," he said.

"Just give me a chance then, okay? To learn?"

Robert nodded.

"*Okay?*"

"Yeah, sure."

"You promise?"

"I promise! Will you stop?"

"Then good. I'm glad it's over. I thought it be a lot worse than it was."

"Whatta you mean?"

"I don't know. I thought you'd walk out on me or somethin'."

"Why? This is even better."

"What is?"

"Nothin'. Just that you are. It's nice."

Jane smiled self-consciously and continued eating. "You know what?" she said, poking her plate with her fork, "the salad here is pretty good."

As they were finishing, a couple in the booth beside them began arguing. The young man pointed at his girlfriend with his fork, and flinging food from his mouth, shouted something indecipherable about dessert. He stopped abruptly, taking deep, exaggerated breaths like a bull about to charge, and without warning, picked up his drink and threw it in his girlfriend's face. He walked out, leaving her with ice in her hair and soda dripping from her nose. Jane offered her napkin. The girl refused, threw money on the table, and ran after him.

"What was that about?" Jane asked.

"Who knows?" Robert said.

"God, I feel so bad."

Jane watched the girl through the window. She was standing alone in the parking lot, wiping her face with her hands, and wiping her hands on her pants. The young man was gone.

Jane and Robert paid separately at Jane's insistence. She joked that he could begin treating her only after they had been more formally introduced. They walked to Robert's car. Jane's body became rigid with expectation. He touched her thigh as he drove.

"A virgin?" he said, teasingly. "We'll fix that."

Jane blushed. "Please, Rob. You promised."

"Don't worry about it."

"I mean, I know I'm ready and all. But what if I need some time to get used to it?"

"I'll handle it," he said.

"Are you sure?"

"Yes, Jane, I'm sure."

"Good," she said, kissing his cheek. "I'm so glad it's with you."

"Me too," he said. "You'll be fine."

He put his hand between her legs.

"Except I'm nervous," she said, squirming away. "I don't know. It feels like we made an appointment. Like I'm going to the doctor's or somethin'."

"You said you trusted me."

"I do!"

"Then will you take it easy?"

"I will, I'm sorry. I'm making it more complicated than it is."

Robert pulled over and put the car in park. "Look, Jane, do you want to or not?" he asked, angrily.

"What? Yes!"

"Then I want you to relax! Okay?"

"I am! Please! Just drive."

They sat silently at a traffic light. "I hate myself," Jane said, finally, playing with the radio. "Please don't be mad. We'll have fun." She rubbed his shoulder.

"Right," he said, returning his hand to her thigh as if to test her. Jane let it stay there and decided that it could go wherever it pleased.

At Durby Street, they entered his apartment. Jane tried to get to the bathroom, but was grabbed by her wrist and escorted to the couch before she had the chance. "No stalling," he said. They kissed and he pulled her shirt above her head, tossing it to the floor beside them. He stood and told her to stand. She listened. He took her pants down and then his own. She felt his fingers inside her, his tongue on her breasts. She asked him to be careful, but playfully. He didn't answer. She closed her eyes and never saw him again.

He spun her around by the shoulders and bent her body over the arm of the couch. He pressed his hand on the small of her back and worked himself inside her. "How's it feel?" he asked her, pulling her hair. "Tell me how's it feel?" He made her tell him she wasn't a virgin anymore. He let go of her hair, bringing both hands to her waist, finishing while she cried into a cushion of ugly brown flowers...

But that was three years ago, or thereabout, and since then, Jane had made up for lost time with plenty of partners, some better, some worse. The past was behind her. She was focused only on Stephen, on making him her own. She was excited by his inexperience, that she could transform him inside her. She had grown confident; she had done it all, and knew how it should be done. She would take care of him.

Jane shifted toward Stephen and tugging him toward her. He rolled his head onto her lap and sprawled across her in what looked like a perverted *Pieta*. He wanted to talk.

"I can't believe I just admitted that to you," he said. "I've never told anyone. It was like, the Pardoner's secret for me."

"Who?"

"From *The Canterbury Tales*...You've heard of it?"

"Sort of."

"Okay, let's just say that if someone ever insinuated I was...you know...I'd be mortified. I leave the room if somebody brings the subject up so I don't have to talk about it."

"Why?"

"Why? 'Cause it's humiliating! I have to pretend like I know what I'm talking about...I'm twenty-one years old!"

"So what? And who was this other guy?" Jane asked.

"What other guy?"

"Pardner."

"Oh! He was some guy who had his secret figured out, that's all."

"But why's it gotta be this a big *secret*? Nobody cares."

"*I* care. I don't think you understand. You have no idea how far it's gone with me. I'm obsessed. Last semester, in an American Literature class—Dr. Ferrara taught it, my hero. Anyway, this girl I liked, she asked me what the reading assignment was. I can't even describe her. She had this flaming red hair—like *The Birth of Venus*. I couldn't believe she was talking to me. I was in shock. I had to be, because I told her. It was an excerpt called *The Dynamo and The Virgin*. My eyes hit the floor when the words came out of my mouth. I was humiliated. I couldn't look at her again."

"She was pretty?" Jane asked, feigning jealousy.

"What? Yeah...like the painting."

"Prettier than me?"

Stephen faltered. "No...no, not really. She—"

"It's ok. You can lie. But I bet she was mean, wasn't she? She wouldn't of understood, like me, would she? Do you know how lucky you are?"

"You're right," Stephen said. "Few girls would have been as patient. Thank you."

"Well, I knew it was something silly," she said, brushing his cheek with the back of her hand. "Why don't you tell me that poem about the moon again?"

"Which one?"

"I don't know. The one you said reminded you of me. About the moon? On her couch?"

"Couch?…Oh, you mean the Baudelaire?"

"I guess."

He recited Baudelaire's *Tristesses de la Lune*. He could only think of Baudelaire when he looked at her, never Yeats, his favorite. He imagined her as his Jeanne Duval. But if it came to pass as he planned, he would one day recite *The Sorrow of Love* to his Maud Gonne.

"Do you want to try again, now that it's out in the open?" she asked, fixing his hair as he finished.

"Yes."

She propped his head and stretched out beside him, a little curtain of flesh, like a *petite* odalisque by Ingres. He was attracted to her like spontaneous tragedy, affected by her like stared-at sun. Surely *this* was the fire he had read about for so long! He held his breath, diving into the dark expanse of her eyes.

She touched his chin with her tongue and whispered in his ear, "It's okay." She placed his hand on her breast and moved it in circles with her own, encouraging him, kissing his neck. She lowered his head with her hand and said softly, "Kiss." She put it in for him and instructed him to strangle her.

Binoculars

The phone rang. Joseph placed his coffee on his *Inquirer*.

"Already he starts," he said, answering. "Hello? Hello? You *motherfuc*ker!"

"I'm gonna kill him, Mag, I swear to God!" he shouted at his wife, Margaret, who was standing behind him. "Saturday morning, he's gotta start. Can't drink your coffee or—"

"Stop it, Joe," Margaret shouted back. "I have a headache."

The crank calls began three weeks ago, courtesy of their daughter's ex-boyfriend. Failing to kill her while with her, he sought redemption by harassing her to death. Joseph signaled the phone company and marked the day and time on a notepad next to the phone. He was building his case for a restraining order.

Joseph had never met him and wished to God that his daughter, Elizabeth, could say the same. During their brief time together, the two of them had conspired to put his family through a season in hell. His wife, exhausted by the effort needed to baby-sit a nineteen-year-old girl, had suffered a nervous breakdown. She had chased after Elizabeth, imprisoned her, fought with her to no avail. The cumulative effect was more than she could take. She was found one night wandering the streets in her bathrobe, searching for Elizabeth's boyfriend with an umbrella. According to her, she was planning to "beat him over the head with it." Doctors admitted her and placed her on anti-depressants. She was getting better, like her old self again, when the phone calls started.

Joseph knew nothing about him but his name, Eddie Zirillo, where he was from, New Jersey, and the other odds and ends his daughter would tell him. She didn't like to talk about it. She referred to that period of her life as her "sickness," which Joseph thought an apt description. Indeed, the very name Zirillo had always sounded to him like a vicious, incurable cancer, for which the only treatment was to wait around as it killed. That Elizabeth survived, he considered miraculous. Yet these unrelenting calls of his were like new clothes on an old stick, a previously unknown strain of the same disease, which threatened relapse in place of remission. Zirillo had never called while he and Elizabeth were a tandem. She wouldn't allow it. She knew her father all too well.

Elizabeth met him while working football games at Veterans Stadium. He bought a hat from her and asked for her phone number. Elizabeth, as if by instinct, asked for his instead. And with that came all this. Joseph marveled at its simplicity. She began, shortly thereafter, to keep unusual hours, sleeping until evening, disappearing until dawn, sometimes returning not at all. She lost her job and unofficially dropped out of the University of Pennsylvania in her second semester. During their frequent fights, she would show up for extended stays, only to lock herself in her room without eating or responding, and to steal from her parents before taking off again. Joseph noticed deep bruises down her arms and suspected more beneath her clothes. He sent Margaret up to search her, and ended up having to separate the ensuing fistfight. She was uncontrollable, and they were helpless. Joseph sometimes stood arms-crossed before his door to prevent Elizabeth from going back to him. She would throw bizarre tantrums, consisting more of songs than screams, and pound her father's chest until Margaret had enough and pushed him out of the way. She even exited from her second story window to escape them. Towards the end, she moved out and vanished completely. Joseph and Margaret wouldn't hear from her again until a phone call from the Methodist Hospital. Elizabeth was found by strangers convulsing on a bench in Marconi Park, five blocks from her house. She never knew how she got there. She had taken, among other things, more xanax than recommended, had her stomach pumped and was saved.

Elizabeth entered rehab, and, to this day, attended meetings. She admitted later to an abortion. Joseph, almost enthusiastically, insisted she had made the right decision. She was diagnosed with trichomonas, Zirillo's final expression of fondness for her, given metronidazole and cured. She got a job at a rare bookstore in Center City. Joseph joked that it was unlikely she'd ever run into Zirillo *there*. She reapplied to school and was accepted. Joseph and Margaret had their daughter back, and congratulated themselves when in bed together that throughout the conflict they had never once given up her. Elizabeth had eluded Zirillo, except, of course, for his phone calls, which began five months after her release from the treatment center.

Joseph heard his daughter's heavy shoes on the hardware floor as she approached the kitchen. She was dressed for work.

"You all right?" he asked, examining her. She appeared as someone still in the early stages of convalescence.

"Yeah. Why?"

"Nothin'. You look beat."

"Do I?" she said. "No, I'm fine. Just tired."

"Didn't you sleep last night?"

"Off and on."

"That's probably why."

"Do I really look bad?"

"No. Just tired. I haven't been sleepin' either." He poured himself a second cup of coffee.

Elizabeth bent over to look in the refrigerator. "So was that him again just now?" she asked.

"Whatta you think?"

She straightened with a carton of orange juice in her hand. "Why is he doing this to me! Can't we change our number?"

"Liz, I told you. I ain't givin' him the satisfaction. That's what he wants. Then he'll figure out the new one and call again. I ain't gonna let it happen."

Elizabeth sighed. "I know, dad, but every time he calls I have to think of his face!"

"Not after Monday you won't. Two more days, he'll be served his papers."

"And then what? I get to see him in court?"

"So? He can't do nothin' to you there. You get to do it to *him* for once."

"Dad, they're not gonna send him to jail for makin' *phone* calls."

"After Monday they will."

Elizabeth shook her head. "I don't think so."

"Trust me, Liz. It's called *harassment*."

"You're sure? Because, really, I can't stand him."

"*You?*"

Elizabeth yanked at a tissue and blew her nose. She grabbed another and blew again. "Maybe we'll get lucky," she said, "maybe he'll just up and die on his own, save us all the trouble."

"I told you about that," Joseph said. "What you gotta do is, you invite him over one day. Tell him me and your mom ain't here. Tell him you wanna talk, like, you're thinkin' about getting' back with him or somethin'. You know he'll come. And when he does, and he's in my house, I'll suddenly fear for my life and the lives of my family, and be forced to defend myself. Right? All I gotta do is show the police the number of calls he's made. I got friends on the force.

Who they gonna believe? They'll see he's dangerous…And that's the end of Eddie Zirillo." He winked at Elizabeth, who laughed at him.

"Joe, I asked you to stop," Margaret intervened, finally. "How many times do I have to tell you? Nobody's killing nobody. I don't want you in jail and I don't want nobody dead. The cops are going to handle this."

Joseph had to listen to the same sermon from his wife every time he threatened "equal consequences" for Zirillo. Margaret had brought home some "cycle of violence" crap with her from therapy that he couldn't understand and didn't want to. It all sounded to him like some recycled phrase from a waiting room pamphlet.

"Oh, but it's okay he almost killed your daughter, right?" he said.

"No, Joe, it's not okay. I want him to go away as much as Liz does, but there's a right and a wrong way to do it. I don't want you to get hurt, or in trouble for hurting him."

"Don't worry 'bout *me* getting hurt."

The phone rang.

"That's it," Elizabeth said. "I'm going to work. I don't even wanna hear it." She kissed her father and ran to the door.

"You want a ride?" Joseph called after her.

"No thanks," she yelled back. Joseph watched the screen door billow shut and the back of her head disappear down the steps. He answered the phone.

"Hello? Hello? You know I'm gonna find you, don't you? You know I'm gonna—You *motherfucker!*"

Margaret stood behind him with a washcloth at her mouth.

"She don't deserve this, Mag. She does not deserve this," he said. "I shoulda taken matters into my own hands a long time ago and never said a word about it."

"And done what?" Margaret said.

"Paid him a visit, that's what. Find out where he lives and introduce myself."

"What good what that do, Joe?"

"More good than a restraining order, I'll tell you that much. We wouldn't be havin' this little repeat performance, now would we? It woulda been over a long time ago. But no. He gets to go on like nothin' happened, call my house, have his fun, while you and Liz are out seein' psychiatrists. It's ain't right. There's gotta be equal consequences."

"We're getting a restraining order," Margaret said carefully. "He's not, 'getting away' with anything."

"So what he can't call anymore? The damage is done. He's laughin' at us. You think he cares about a restraining order?"

"For the last time, Joe, we're going to the cops. If they can't help us, then you can do whatever you want. But at least give them a chance first."

"Whattaya *think* I'm doin'? All I'm sayin' is, one day, when he forgets all about Elizabeth, and he has his hands on some other girl, I'm gonna pay him a visit. *I'm* not gonna forget. He will, but I won't."

"Fine. Just not now." Margaret would deal with that when the time came.

"You're the only thing stoppin' me, Mag, 'cause I know for a fact Elizabeth wouldn't care. Trust me. She tells me everyday how she feels." He marked the phone call on his notepad. "How could you blame me for wantin' to kill this kid?"

"I don't...Please. There are better ways...Do it for me?"

"I am," he said.

When Elizabeth was in rehab, and even afterward, Joseph had rejected the idea of getting even with Zirillo. He didn't want to draw him back into her life. He wanted time to distance her from the events before retaliating on her behalf. Then the phone rang, just as things began to reacquire the feel of before, and Joseph's more tactful considerations were abandoned in favor of "paying him a visit." It grew worse with each call. Joseph stomped about the kitchen, raving like Ahab to the sound of the dial tone. Margaret had to leave the room. It became his obsession, metastasizing until finally he asked Elizabeth for Zirillo's address. She couldn't remember the number or the street, but knew it began with a W, *Wist* something, she said, somewhere in Turnersville, New Jersey. Joseph's threats to confront Zirillo then met suddenly with complete and unexpected opposition from his wife, who had squealed his intentions to her therapist, and, according to Joseph, had been "brainwashed" against them. They argued outside Elizabeth's hearing and reached a compromise.

Joseph consulted his attorney, Mr. Connel, an older man in a tighter shirt, who advised him to "document all calls" and, after a certain number, to file for a restraint, at which time Zirillo would be subpoenaed and Elizabeth would have her day in court. Much to Joseph's dismay, Margaret was thrilled with the idea. Mr. Connel, who had drawn certain conclusions due to Joseph's colorful account of Zirillo's character, advised him to keep his distance, that retaliation of any kind would jeopardize his case. "You sound like my wife," Joseph sneered, and gave his word to both of them that he would use "only the proper channels." Though he intended to note Zirillo's calls, as promised, he had decided upon a more Machiavellian maneuver to have his number traced in secrecy. As a result, he had been carrying Zirillo's address in his wallet for a week.

Having never seen Zirillo, he couldn't resist taking a ride to his house. He needed to know whom he was up against. He left the refinery on Friday night and drove to Wisteria Road in Turnersville, swearing he would do nothing more than look. After all, Margaret had yet to outlaw *looking* at Zirillo. Wisteria Road, however, thwarted his plans.

It was more of a circular stretch of highway separated from Zirillo's house by fifty yards of grass. A paved ramp cut through the field and led to his driveway. Joseph couldn't see, and, not wanting to drive to Zirillo's front door, decided on a return trip Saturday morning.

Joseph finished his paper and coffee. He hurried through a shower and got dressed.

"Did he call while I was in there?" he asked Margaret, returning to the kitchen.

"God, Joe, will you let it drop? Either he's calling or you're complaining about it. I don't know which is worse. I haven't had a moment's peace in three weeks."

Joseph let it drop and went digging in his back cellar. In the crate beside the water heater, buried beneath mummers plaques and trophies from Elizabeth's dance recitals, he found his binoculars. He put them around his neck. The phone rang upstairs. He waited for his wife to answer. To hell with it, he thought. He opened a closet, reached into the inside pocket of a leather jacket and pulled out his .38. He hadn't seen it for some time. Joseph studied the handle, the trigger, the barrel, before unloading it to avoid temptation. He wanted to pistol whip Zirillo once for every phone call. That seemed about right. To hell with a restraining order, and Mr. Connel, and Margaret, and the "proper channels"—this was more gratifying. This was for Elizabeth. He had listened to Margaret, had weighed her point of view, and concluded that both his *and* her plan could be carried out. Zirillo, after all, had yet to meet *him*. He would approach him as a stranger, hope Zirillo could read between the lines, and, adding insult to injury, press charges all the same. It would stay between the two of them. He'd send Margaret to court with Elizabeth, tell them he was "afraid of what he might do if he saw him." He doubted Zirillo would even attend. They'd probably never even see each other again. He put the binoculars under his shirt and under his armpit, and the empty gun in the waist of his pants.

"Was it him?" he asked, coming upstairs.

"No," Margaret answered. "It was my sister."

"What did she want?"

"Nothing. I said I'd call her back." She looked exhausted, like before. The calls were unnerving her, and he wasn't helping by making her worry, needlessly. He changed his mind. He would only look.

"Did you see my keys?" he asked.

"They're right there."

"Where?"

"Right in front of you." She pointed to a counter-top.

Joseph found them and scooped them up. "I'll be back," he said.

"Where you goin'?"

"To the store. You need anything?"

"We need milk."

"That's right. I'll get it."

Joseph kissed her on the forehead. "Monday, Mag. It'll all be over." She was silent.

"Just mark it down if he does call," he said.

He dropped the gun in his golf bag by the door. He put his sunglasses on and walked to his car. Someone had double-parked him in.

"God*damm*it!" He pounded the roof of his car with his fist, then entered the bakery on the corner.

"Does anybody own the red jeep outside?" he shouted. "It's blocking me in." There was quite a commotion. The customers shuffled in line as if collectively accused. They bumped shoulders with each other, whispering "red jeep," trying to remember which color and type of vehicle they owned and whether or not they had driven it to the bakery.

"That's me! I'm coming," a young girl said from the counter, receiving her change.

The crowd let her pass. An old lady clicked her tongue at her in contempt. She and Joseph walked out together. She was about Elizabeth's age, heavyset and pretty. She wore a baseball cap with a ponytail swinging from the opening in the back.

"I'm sorry," she said. "I thought I could get away with it."

"Forget it. It's nothin'."

"I only wanted a dozen rolls. I didn't expect the line to be so long."

"Yeah, it's a madhouse on Saturdays."

"You ever get your rolls in there?" she asked.

"Of course. I live right down the street."

"They make great rolls, don't they?"

"The best."

"And their stromboli's good too."

"Ham and cheese," he recommended.

"Omygod, I love their ham and cheese!"

Joseph was impressed. "You got good taste."

"What about the garlic bread?" she asked.

"Ah, the garlic bread. Can't beat it."

"Omygod, I know! It's *so* good."

They stopped at the curb in front of Joseph's car.

"Well, I'll see ya!" she said. "It was nice meeting you…"

"Joe."

"Joe. I'm Nancy." They shook hands.

"Nice to meet ya, Nancy."

"Sorry 'bout blockin' you in."

"Don't worry about it." Joseph got into his car and started it, following Nancy out of the parking space. She waved to him in her rear view mirror. He honked his horn twice and waved back.

Traffic was light on the Walt Whitman Bridge, allowing Joseph an uninterrupted ride to Wisteria Road. He pulled over to the shoulder of the road and put his blinkers on. Placing his sunglasses on the dashboard, he took the binoculars from under his shirt and lifted them to his eyes, viewing the inside of Zirillo's living room between opened yellow curtains, the only curtains that weren't closed. He saw a lamp without a shade on a table next to a turned-off television, and the footrest of a stretched recliner, though nobody's feet were using it. "Can't even close up a chair," Joseph mumbled, tuning the radio to the oldies station. He reminded himself to get milk and something else.

Kids were playing football on the field in front of Zirillo's house, using the paved path to their driveways as an end zone. The high sun shed kaleidoscopically through an eclipse of trees, as players disappeared into and emerged out of the slow-dancing shadows, which twirled across the enormous lawn, choreographed by the wind.

Joseph knew he was home. He had called twice that morning. Three times if Margaret was lying about her sister. He started to root for one of the football teams, raising the binoculars at the end of every play. An hour passed before someone entered the room. Joseph opened his eyes wide against the lenses of the binoculars, batting his eyelashes out of the way. A young man stood shirtless in front of the television with a remote control in his hand. His hair was pulled back in a ponytail. He smoked casually, flicking ashes on the floor. "You sonovabitch," Joseph said.

Joseph had always been able, eventually, to beat back the outrage Zirillo caused him. He was more idea than actual, an evil known only in name, doubted until seen, something against which Joseph was helpless to retaliate. But now that he had an image, finally, around which his hatred could rally, it nearly devoured him. He thought of Elizabeth, how he had held her hand and with his thumb, had gently brushed the tape holding her intravenous in place following the overdose. He thought of his gun and wished he had brought it. More than ever, he wanted to introduce himself to Zirillo. He watched as Zirillo picked up a phone next to the lamp, dialed, waited, and hung up. "You *motherfuck*er!" he screamed, punching his steering wheel, accidentally hitting the horn. He raised the binoculars again. Zirillo was laughing, talking to someone in another room. Joseph waited, and through his binoculars watched as Elizabeth walked in the room.

A Simple Solution

His sister called him home to talk. She wouldn't say over the phone. She wanted to meet with him face-to-face in the playground at the corner of their street.

He was sitting on the middle bench of three at the sideline of an empty basketball court. The rims had been torn down by neighborhood kids to keep the black kids from playing. There were mouth-holes in both backboards and cracks in the concrete at center court. He lit a cigarette and waited. November's comfortable, contemplative shroud had cornered the gray sky and descended. It was a chaffing autumn afternoon. Sunlight streaked through the sifting clouds and was fractured into separate shafts like channels stretched from ground to sky. A dog barked behind him. He turned as it detonated a throng of pigeons into flight. He looked at his watch. She was late. To pass the time, he read the graffiti scrawled across the back of the bench.

Joe D. fucked Maria Galuccio right here. There was actually an arrow pointing to where his sister would be sitting. He spread his arms in a gesture of disbelief and moved to the bench to his left. Joe D. had yet to make a landmark of it. He focused on a pair of flies circling the carcass of an eaten apple at the base of a trashcan.

He saw his sister crossing at the corner. The slanted light elongated her shadow in the street like mystery and melancholy. She entered through the front fence, waving as she walked.

"Hi," she said, sitting down.

"Hello."

"Sorry I had to call you here."

"Don't worry about it."

"God! She's everywhere!"

"Who?"

"Mommy. You can't even talk in that house. I hate it."

"That's why I left," he said.

"Yeah, well, you're lucky. I can't wait. You got any cigarettes?"

He gave her one, struck and cupped a match for her.

"What's that word you used to use for her?" she asked. "The long word?"

"Ubiquitous?"

"That's the one!" she said, pointing at him.

He hadn't seen her since he moved away. He looked her over, and, as always, thought her faultless. She possessed a chameleon-like beauty, capable of transmuting the world around her, making beautiful even the weeds among which she sat. Incredulous strangers would pause when she passed, needing a moment to differentiate their dreams from her reality. Her long, red hair surpassed the tiny circumference of her waist, giving the pretty impression from afar of a girl engulfed in flames. She was rare and she was beautiful, cursed to attract everything amidst the toppled towers of a ruin. She was love in a place of excrement.

"So," he said, "how awful is it?"

"How awful's what?"

"What you're about to tell me?"

"I don't know," she said, scratching her arm.

"Because if it's about him, I already know."

"Know what?"

"That you're back together."

She lowered her eyes.

"Aren't you?" he asked.

She answered matter-of-factly, "Yes."

"You didn't have to drag me all the way down here for that."

"How did you know?"

"'Cause that's how it always happens. You'll break up with him twenty more times before it sticks. It's a cycle of false starts. Like quitting smoking. And anyway, your tone of voice gave it away last time we talked. It was kind of obvious."

"I was scared though," she said, as if pleading with him.

"Scared of what?"

"You know."

"No I don't know."

"That he'd kill himself."

He made a face. "Do you know why I never called you back that night to ask you what happened?"

"Why?"

"Because I knew."

"Knew what?"

"That he wasn't going to kill himself. I told you. Guys like him never do. He'd be doing us all a favor and he knows it. He'll live forever out of spite."

"But you didn't hear him on the phone," she said. "He was serious."

"Was he? Then you should have encouraged him."

"How can you say that?"

"Why not? What are you supposed to do? Ruin your life to save his?"

"No. But I didn't want him to die."

"So you'll kill yourself instead?"

"I'm not killing myself," she said.

He shot a glance over the periodic horizon, abbreviated by rows of rooftops. The earlier clouds had faltered and a spider sun was again at prey above a sprawling gutter, reflecting off the chain-link fence that surrounded them like the barbed wire of a prison yard.

"This is what I tried to tell you, that you won't comprehend," he said as though to say it pained him. "He isn't going to die. At least not by his own hands. You're being held hostage. Really, what right does he have to place the burden of his existence on you?" He thought of a poem to illustrate the point, but willed it away. She wouldn't understand.

"Think about it," he continued. "He forced you to love him, whether you love him or not, because if you don't, he'll blow his brains out? In your name. Is that it?"

"No. I mean no, because I *do* love him."

"Who are you trying to convince?"

"Whattaya mean?"

"Look, all I know is, he threatened to kill himself and you believed he would and now, I think, you're with him solely to prevent it. You're being exploited. And it's an old trick." He took a deep breath and tried a different tack. "You were separated for a month, right? And you life was in order again, wasn't it?"

"Yes."

"Then what happened? Why'd you make a mess of it again?"

"I didn't," she said. "I just didn't want him to kill himself. Not over *me*. I didn't want it to be my fault. I wouldn't be able to live with myself if I was the reason, when I coulda did something and saved him."

He made a face.

"Stop making faces!" she yelled at him.

"I'm sorry. I'm having a hard time understanding. Why is it your job to save him? Since when do *you* have to be someone else's reason for living?"

She covered her face with her hands. He realized that for the past two years the two of them had ceased to *talk*. Instead, he lectured and she listened, or he accused and she defended herself, or he pleaded and she made promises.

"Look at what he's saying to you," he said, gently. "Love me and let me ruin your life. If you don't, I'll kill myself…and ruin your life. It's all he has to offer."

"But it's changed, though," she said, taking her hands from her face.

He laughed. "You drive me crazy, you know that?"

"Wait. Listen," she said, blushing. "Ever since that phone call, when he threatened to do it, things have been different. Whether you believe it or not."

His hands fell noisily to his lap. "I give up," he shrugged. "It was a threat! Can't you see? There was never any intent!"

"But I heard the gun! He *was* serious. You weren't on the phone. You don't know. And that's not why I took him back, either. I just wanted to stop it before it happened. I wanted to calm him down and talk him out of it."

"Instead he talked you into it?"

"No! He said that for the first time in his life he knew what his life was like if I was gone and he wouldn't risk it again."

"You didn't roll your eyes at that?"

"Stop it!"

"Seriously, I could have told you word for word what he'd say."

He stared at two dogs chasing each other in an enclosed area behind the basketball court and at their owners talking at the outside gate, holding leashes.

"Everybody deserves a second chance," she said.

"He used his second chance twenty chances ago, don't you think?"

"No. 'Cause they were little things. He made that one big mistake and he apologized for it and it's over with and it's different now and everybody just has to deal with it." She took a breath.

"How's it different?" he asked, aggressively. He was tired of listening to her enumerate the virtues of a liar and a cheat. "He made you take him back at gun point. Is that different? It's exactly like him. You're not his mother. You're not responsible for what he does with the rest of his life, and you're certainly not responsible if he chooses to end it, which he won't. And believe me, even if he did, and even if he called out your name as he did it, it wouldn't be your fault. The kid has deep-seated problems he isn't even aware of. What he wants is a scapegoat and he's found one."

"You don't understand!"

"*I* don't?"

"No! When somebody you love has a gun to his head it isn't so easy to just hang up the phone and let them do it."

"What if the only option they give you is to spend the rest of your life pretending you're still in love with them? What else are you supposed to do?"

"I'm not pretending," she said.

"You're afraid of him. That's why you're with him."

"Can I have another cigarette?" she asked, sighing.

He gave her one, struck and cupped a match for her.

"Listen," he said. "I know better than you think. I grew up on these corners. I know them all already. I know him. I've met him a thousand times. He's manipulative and you're an easy target 'cause you're young and he knows it and he knows what to do with it. You're not the first. And as long as you're his, and even for a long while afterward, you won't be able to have a life of your own. Trust me, next time he'll threaten to kill *you*, or he'll ask you to kill yourself for him, all because he hates himself and he hates his life and he hates and resents and wants to take it all out on you. This is love to him. He has no idea what it is."

"Do you?" she said. "When were you in love? You like to talk about it."

He was silent.

"I'm sorry," she said.

"I've been in love," he said. "And that's not the point."

"I didn't mean it."

"Forget it. What I want to know is, have you ever considered that the world is a much bigger place than South Philly? And that you've yet to see any of it?"

"Not really," she answered without considering.

"Well you should because it is. And of all the men you've yet to meet, your heart is set on *him*? Can't you imagine someone else? Something better?"

"I'm happy the way it is."

"Then it's settled," he said. "It's the same thing, over and over again. You know what? You're right, it's your life. You can make it beautiful or you can spoil it or you can let him spoil it, I can't do anything for you. If you want to be with him, fine. I want no parts of it."

"See!" She slapped the bench between them.

"What?"

"You sound just like them."

"Like who?"

"Like mommy and daddy."

"How?" He was insulted.

"They hate him too," she said.

"Can you blame them?"

"No. But that's the problem. That's why I called you here. Because of them."

"What about them?"

"They won't let me see him! All of a sudden. It was fine before then. Then we broke up and I told mommy some of what happened and now they don't want me to see him no more." She was sobbing. "They make me sneak around and I hate it. He can't call. I can't bring him into the house. He can't even walk me home! You know how that makes me feel? What else could I do?"

He put his arm around her. "Why can't it be like before?" she said, composing herself. "I have to meet him on the street or in some scuzzy apartment. Do you think I wanna do that? Do you know how that makes me feel? I hate it."

He couldn't talk. He held her close to him. The compressed row homes gloated at him from across the street. He looked above them, into an evacuated sky, and wanted to rally a riot of lightning powerful enough to abort the deformity beneath it. All which his child's mistake fancied as lost had been stored for him at home.

He felt her chest convulsing against his own. "I didn't know what else to do," she sniffed over his shoulder. "I had to do something. I hate it when I'm alone! It's like, now I'm not even a part of my family no more."

"I don't know what else to tell you," he said, hopelessly. "What can you do?" He followed a little boy as he chased another into the playground and past their bench. They caught up with each other eventually and wrestled on a patch of grass.

She pulled back and looked at them and then into his eyes, heaving. Her eyes were disheveled and swollen, yet her beauty delighted in disorder.

"I only wanted him to be accepted," she said. "And I didn't know how else."

"I don't think they ever will," he said.

"No, 'cause I know them."

"Who? Mom and dad?"

"Yes."

"What about them?"

"They would never."

"Never what?"

She brushed her hair from her mouth. The wind had been wrapping it around her face and toying with it throughout. "It was the most simplest way I could think of," she said.

"*What* was?" he said, bothered by her mistake.

She searched the ground at her feet. "I didn't know how else," she nearly whispered. "I wanted them to accept him."

"I don't understand what you're saying," he said, confused.

"I had to. So I did."

"Did *what*?" His confusion lingered for a moment before his heart snapped, and he understood.

"You didn't," he said, wincing. "Did you?"

She didn't answer.

He turned her face to his and asked again, *"Did you?"*

Confession, etc.

Ah, there you are. Please, please, sit down. What's that? No, not at all. Though I *have* already ordered. Yes, the soup, I know. Your favorite…So, how have you been? Really! I'd been meaning to ask. It's been how long now since you've graduated? *Three years!* Already? Yes, you're right, I retired shortly thereafter. Next semester, I think—was it?—yes, I think it was. My, but where *are* the snows, etc.?…Hmm? Oh, yes, certainly, be my guest. Nothing's too good for my *protégé*. Do you remember how I called you that? No, don't be shy. You're living up to it. The poems you talk about, they sound, well, *remarkable*. Have you written them yet? No, it was nothing. I'm glad I could help, that's all. It was but a simple suggestion. What's that? *Why* have I asked you here? Oh, I don't know, but some things are better said *face-to-face*. Those letters of ours, so…*impersonal*, don't you think? No, you're right. Forgive me, please, it will all be made clear quite soon…We'll speak in Literature, yes? Good. I don't want the *brutes* to overhear us.

How should I begin?…Let's just say, it's about a new work of mine. No, it's unfinished…but close. I want to tell you about it, and, also, something else…Perhaps we should go then, you and I, etc., to the source…

It was during a low-point in an age of widespread Romantic folly, that an English Opium-Eater, famous for his confessions, raised a great *hubbub* over the significance of a knock on a gate. Do you follow? Good…The English Opium-Eater, you see, deemed it yet another example of a mighty poet's infallibility by claiming that this incongruous event served both to wrench an audience out of sympathy with a murderer and to reflux the human upon the fiendish, etc. Of course, the mighty poet chuckles at all this. He was, in fact, attempting nothing more than to make a pit full of ruffians drool on themselves in effort to recapture their attention spans, which a brilliant and therefore undesired parenthesis had suspended, by unleashing a litter of bad puns and crude jokes on the correlation between drunkenness and impotence, etc. The mighty poet, as you know, quite often kowtows to the uncouth out of virtuous necessity.

As a result, we may wish everlasting farewell to the English Opium-Eater and his fantastical display of a most *unfounded* extrapolation. Its vision has long been blurred, and its endurance has long embarrassed a host of worthier critics, myself included.

I must also insist, as a preemptive disclaimer, that you do not mistake my assessment, correct though it may be, as an expression of *jealousy* on my part, as a mean-spirited swipe at a piece of criticism I wish for myself. I could not possibly be so *frivolous*. The threat of blindness is a constant one, and throughout my tenure I have considered myself to be, first and foremost, an *optometrist*. After all, am *I* to blame if the English Opium-Eater had been ingesting, no, *indulging* prior to the composition of his essay? My modesty, however, precludes my stooping to such pettiness.

What does "all this" have to do with anything? Quite a lot, I'm afraid. You see, I've pointed out "all this" only to cite precedent. For I, too, have fiddled with doors, not to mention opium, during the course of my, until now, *undistinguished* career as critic, and I have drawn more successful, no, more *logical* conclusions. (Undistinguished, that is, except for a brief and minor triumph, before your time, when I caused quite a stir by proving, mathematically, that the Moor of Venice was justified. But never mind.) Where was I? Ah, yes, doors. I should first tell you that my agenda here is twofold. First, I wish to give you a synopsis of the work by which I shall conquer my discipline, as they say, "once and for all." I have rectified an *assumed* interpretation of a classic with an idea that ne'er was thought nor ne'er before expressed in either prose or rhyme. Secondly, by doing so, I wish to honor tradition by setting before you an individual talent in all the truth of nature, etc. In short, I must confess.

I have been patient long enough, but beware the fury of a patient man! I have suffered slings and arrows in outrageous silence, forever tarrying, forced by fate to be a kind of *Raphael without arms*, though I have done so secretly scoffing, in possession of something enormous, which, only now, fearing that I may cease to be, do I elect to share. Enlightenment must, I suppose, reach even the darkest shores. Ahem.

From my boyish days I had always felt a great perplexity on one point in *C&P*. It was this: While attending to the pawnbroker's head with his axe, Rodion *absentmindedly* leaves the door to her flat "unfastened and at least six inches open. No lock, no bolt, all the time, all that time!" It must be pointed out, if you are unfamiliar, that Rodion's estimation is incorrect. The door is *actually* left "at least six inches open" by his second, unexpected victim, upon returning to her sister's with that mysterious "bundle." One may conjecture that *she* enters through a door left *wide open* by Raskolni—I mean, Rodion. You never can be too sure what the primates have read, you know? Anyway, this produced to my feelings an effect for which I could never account.

This "detail of the open door" has been consistently overlooked, and with good reason: it can be very easily explained away; and easy explanations, you'll find, are what critics everywhere crave. The conventional take (and I am ashamed to propound it further, if only to eradicate it) blathers on about the unmatched intensity of Literature's most powerful scene, of which the open door is "but another component," or reduces the door to a symbolic "source" of Rodion's delirium. There are others who assure us that Rodion is, at best, a third-rate criminal, a great *bungler*, incapable of crime, an individual far too sensitive and all together devoid of the heartlessness required to tap-dance in puddles of blood without being overtaken by self-loathing. His momentary lapse, therefore, is simply the first in a series of false starts and amateur over-sights committed before, during, and after the crime as examples of his overall ineptitude. Rodion, they—Hold on! Let me finish…

Rodion, they continue, is not only unfit to be criminal, but, more cuttingly, to be a "Superman" as well. Having put twice two together, they conclude, not without a measure of pride, I'm sure, that the Author, as he is wont to do with his atheists, is making a mockery of poor Rodion Romanovich throughout the scene by providing an ironic juxtaposition of the man and his philosophy, as if to say, "Look at this pathetic spectacle, would you? Here, gentlemen, is your Superman, who defies, no, *transcends* the Universal Laws of Morality! Here is your man of Genius, who, take note, fails to close the door behind him as he murders, who is subject to the same childish and phenomenal heedlessness he had earlier denounced in 'lesser' men!" Worst of all, and proper insult escapes me, there are those who take Rodion at his word, when he accounts for the blunder by blaming *his victim*, who, he contends, had not shut the door, "per-haps as a precaution." Now explain to me how such critics could fail to recog-nize so obvious an evasion as Raskolnikov's way of saying, "Certainly *I* could not have been so stupid!" What's that? I did? Well, it was bound to slip *eventu-ally*. Do you think they heard me? No? Good. Now where was I?…Ah, yes, stu-pidity.

Don't you see? That he very well *could* have been so stupid? And such lazy explanations for a seemingly minute detail have been declared satisfactory by a swarm of counterfeiters, as incompetent and unskilled as the crime they critique, who, for forty-some years now, I've had the ugly misfortune of calling colleagues. Could there be a greater want of skill? Yes, very good, 'tis hard to say. The most *I* can do is sigh, a little sadly, that ever I was born to set it right! But what—Pardon? Uh, yes, another glass will be fine. You? Yes, he'll have another as well, thank you…These outdoor cafes, so, *Parisian*. You know, They say Paris is beautiful in spring, though I doubt it when I see all *this*. But Philadelphia truly is a *gutter*, isn't it? Yes, yes, I know, looking at the stars, etc. Do you believe I've spent a lifetime here? Don't get me wrong, I pride myself on a rather *cosmopolitan* past…Yet I always come home again. Why? What is it about this place that keeps us here? Gr-r-r—how it sickens me! Where would I be without my books? The city is a cage. What's Alexandria compared to it? But I digress…

Where were we? No, don't tell me. I'll remember…Greater want of skill…Hard to say…Yes, there it is—What, then, is the truth? If our Rodya is a third-rate criminal, it is because his Author is a first-rate Artist, who would never play at dice, who would never be so *frivolous* with open doors. If it were only as simple as it appears, and if only Raskolnikov knew, standing there, in a room with an unanticipated view, that, in the end, *he did not have a choice.*

The idea first occurred to me seventeen years ago, while my wife, Antonia—do you hear the name?—Di'*Aretino* and I were vacationing in another country. Ah, I remember it well! My beloved! She was younger than I, a former student. She was like an aria sung behind a dream of white mules and whirlwinds. (Yes, that *is* how I put it. This was, understand, during my Symbolist days, since abandoned.) Antonia, she had the manners of a duchess then, with a heart so—how shall I say it—so very *glad*. She was leopard-limbed, untethered, enough to agitate archangels faithless, to lure them into the Devil's party without their knowing it. She was a woman high and low…Why I never told you? Well, let's just say, she is difficult to discuss.

I was in Italy on sabbatical, writing an essay on "Eternal Symbols" in literature, since abandoned. I had just finished a section in praise of that scene in which the life of a famous first line is saved by, of all things, a coffin, and was relaxing on a lawn chair beneath the busy old fool. You follow? Good. A whale of a book, isn't it? As I was saying. I was reading the opening chapters of a rather *defunct* novel from a would-be poet concerning the fate of two very different women, sisters, I believe, each a symbol of something prosaic and certainly not eternal, who were in love with, unbeknownst to them, two closeted homosexuals, one a violent brute, the other an insufferable bore. What's that?

Yes, David Herbert. Hmm? You *liked* it? Sometimes I worry about you. Nonetheless. Am I being unusually obtuse, or do men very often wrestle naked? It's unimportant. What is important, however, is something he wrote to the effect that, "There is no such thing as pure accident. Everything that happens has a universal significance. It all hangs together, in the deepest sense." He even went so far as to claim that a man cannot be murdered unless he *desires* to die!

I dropped the book to think about it. Though it made immediate sense, I could not immediately grasp its *outward* significance. As I continued contemplating, I was interrupted by Antonia, who was giggling at me from the balcony above. Over what, exactly, I don't know. It was a habit of hers. It was her *humor*. I mention it only because at the very moment I looked up, I noticed the door leading back to her bedroom left *wide open* behind her, and thought instinctively of our Rodka in the new light of this new idea, when, as unlikely as all that, it came to me, an entire theory! Ah, but here is our food. Me? Why, the *fra diablo*, of course. As always, yes. No, eat, eat. By the way, how *is* Mademoiselle Lescaut? Yes, your *mistress*. You have "saved" her, as you write, have you not? I'd been meaning to ask...*Is* she? Good, good...And your jealousy? It is, *under control*? I agree, that is *most* important...Now surely you can eat and listen at the same time, yes?...Very well.

For obvious reasons, as previously stated and as you shall presently see, I have been required—are you listening?—to shelter my *illumination* from a *darkling plain* where ignorant armies, etc. But now, as my way of life falls deep into a dry month, and I await the rain with trousers rolled, in possession of neither world enough nor time (I could go on forever), I present, past due, a somewhat *abridged* explication of the open door. My lute, awake! Hail, Muse! *et cetera*.

Since it must be said, once, at least, allow me to whisper his name: *Rodion Romanovich Raskolnikov*—the most complete psychological creation since a blown youth was blasted with ecstasy—is a man whose subconscious is in an uproar; yet, throughout the novel, we are permitted only those thoughts of which he is *conscious*. Even as the crime is newly consummated, he wants, no, *needs* to be caught—of this much we are sure, even if we don't know why (Porphiry knows all too well). How many times, after all, does he come close to confessing, even initiating contact with the police, whenever it appears as though he will get off scot-free if only he'd just keep his mouth shut? And how many times, really, can one man faint at the mere mention of murder? What has been lost in translation, though, is Rodion's pursuit of punishment even *before* he has conceived of his crime. The very title of the book should be reversed—*Punishment and Crime!* Rodya does not concoct a plan to murder, but rather, a plan for Siberia, *predicated* upon murder. In short, it is no mistake, no *accident*. Raskolnikov has conveniently, no, *strategically* allowed an open door to go unshut *on purpose*. He is at the mercy of a will unknown to him, but entirely his own, a will to be persecuted, to eat cabbage and cockroaches in the House of the Dead, and our first glimpse of this hidden desire is given through the open door. You look doubtful…I'll explain.

There was a French Mathematician and Religious Bookmaker, famous for his *thoughts*, who, long ago, set the odds for a now classic gambling proposition in which the existence of God was ventured. Quite logically, he analyzed the pros and cons of each side and ultimately concluded not only the safest but also the most obvious bet, and demanded that we, if rational, wager likewise. Again, I bring up "all this" only to cite precedent. Raskolni—Rodion, by means of murder, makes an even more lucrative wager of a similar sort, demanding more immediate results and accepting *only* those results to his liking. He wants to collect *in this life*, and, we find out, is a sore loser.

He is prone to paint himself Promethean with revolt, and critics everywhere have fallen for his *Napoleonic* posturing. The truth, they will be shocked to learn, is that he has risked a life's savings on an outcome that is directly opposed to the high-minded theories with which he seems obsessed, and that his ends, to critical dismay, never know their beginnings. He brings the axe to the pawnbroker's head, you see, with a *rooting interest*, namely, for a stint in Siberia. But why?

Raskolnikov is a desperate man in the midst of a crisis. Mad Russia has hurt him into poverty. He is too intelligent, too *deserving*, for a place as dismal, as stupid as Petersburg. He is neither an avowed truth-seeker nor a dedicated metaphysician (unlike myself). If he were, murder would resemble science. It would have been *experimental*, done to dissect. The axe would have invaded the old lady's head with the strictest objectivity, with the same professionalism exhibited by a chemist in the lab. But poor Rodion isn't any more a scientist than he is a criminal. Much like the Author himself, Raskoln—ah, to hell with it, what do they know?—Ras*k*olnikov is a *gambler*…and is on a losing streak.

He suffers from what the world may one day call, (which I have already, note, taken the liberty to call) "metaphysical schizophrenia," a disease epidemic to our late century, and heralded by Raskolnikov, whose Creator was always more prophet than man. Raskolnikov suspects, God forbid, that God is dead, and that, consequently, he has acquired the right to "play God," yet he abhors this right and wishes to prove his suspicions false. There is only one way: he must murder to find out for sure.

Raskolnikov takes it upon himself to play a game of (again, my own term), "spiritual roulette," with the destiny of his soul at stake. He will either be saved or condemned by his action. The rules are simple. If Raskolnikov is apprehended and punished for his crime, then God's in his heaven and all's right with the world! His faith in Moral Law and Divine Retribution will, much to his relief, be restored. Thus, he neither defies nor transcends morality, but rather *invokes* it to demonstrate its reality. Punishment indicates an ordered, meaningful universe, operating according to immutable laws and governed by design even in a thing so small, in short, exactly what our Rodya wants. Freedom, on the other hand, though soaked in blood, would corroborate God's nonexistence, and convict the universe of being orderless, meaningless, an expense of spirit in a waste, etc., where anything goes and everything is permitted. On one side there is Prison and the Infinite, on the other, Freedom and Nothingness; and Rodion is sure of one thing: that God will speak, that he will appear, somehow, in the machine. What? Yes, for Christ's sake, everything is fine! Will you leave us be? Thank you…The fop!

Where was I? Ah, yes. As the book begins, *in the middle of things*, on that exceptionally hot evening in early July, Raskolnikov's subconscious has already placed its chips, though the spur of his true intent is withheld from us until the open door. He does not murder to achieve the extraordinary, as he *thinks*, but to confirm that the ordinary is well and as it should be; he does not murder to rid humanity of a pestilential old hag (Lord knows, there are too many), but to return it, through her sacrifice, to an evicted divinity; he does not murder to become God, but to become more fully human in his knowledge of an assertive and, above all, *accessible* God. (And isn't *that* what humanity has always sought? A Holy Spirit cast in the image of Parrot rather than Dove? Something capable of response, even *self-induced* response? They are simple hearts, are they not?)

Rodya's seeming repudiation of God, his awful *daring* of a moment's etc., is more of a screaming out to Him in His maddening invisibility to stand and unfold Himself, to give, as it were, "a sign" that He is watching, that He is displeased—as if God could be goaded by sin or courted by blasphemy. It is a reframing of that tale first told by the Idiot himself, namely, "Why have you forsaken me?" Raskolnikov has bet unscrupulously on what he hopes to be a sure thing, and sets the wheel in motion with murder. But when it appears that an unlikely upset has occurred, that he and God have gone equally bankrupt, what does he do? He fixes the game in their favor as if to say, "best two out of three!"

Raskolnikov's subsequent delirium is the result of guilt, not that he has murdered, as most would have you believe, but of guilt that he has *yet to be found guilty of murder.* His subconscious, finally, has come teething to the surface. It becomes increasingly clear to our Rodya that his bluff has been called, and that now he must level with a nightmare—playing God in a godless world. He talked the part, of course, because he never dreamed the day would come. His essays on morality are written merely to *instigate* the act, to conjure the courage equal to, etc. Following his crime, he lives as though expecting, any day now, to be incinerated by a bolt from Heaven. On the contrary, God is implacable, conspicuously silent, and Raskolnikov, knowing what this entails and fearing it, acts as ventriloquist, places words in God's mouth, which, mind you, *may have never come,* and does everything in his power to facilitate a "response" in order to get himself caught. Even then, God does not speak, and Raskolnikov is inclined to take it a step further, to wear his confession like a scarlet *M* stitched to his rags, leaving him no choice but to turn himself in, to take to his "cross" (at the bidding of a whore no less), according to what he believes is *God's will.* The subconscious will out. It is Raskolnikov's way of pulling back from an awful parenthesis, of resetting things to normal. God is in His Heaven once again, whether He is or He isn't. Finding out for sure has become too sick an enterprise. The horror, not of losing God, but of *sensing* the loss (a more vicious exponent of mere *suspicion*), is enough to convince Raskolnikov that God necessarily exists. Thus, a murder, done at first for proof, becomes, by book's end, reclamation of blind faith. Raskolnikov does not confess, he *quits.*

Is this not the most wonderful neurosis ever imagined? He doubts God, murders to expel it, and frames himself when doubt seems justified! For doubt is Raskolnikov's *true* crime, murder his punishment, and Siberia his means of redemption for the sin of *uncertainty.* The door is left ajar, you see, because never once, from the first page forward, does Raskolnikov expect to live freely, "beyond Good and Evil," with not only murder but the meaninglessness of life itself on his conscience. He would have killed himself first (as the Author's atheists are wont to do; see: Svidrigailov, who comes close).

Raskolnikov is, of course, a failure, as is his attempt at proof. His tampering with evidence proves nothing, really, except to himself. At best, he manages to reinforce a fading illusion by a most perverted method. Wagering everything on red, he stops the wheel mid-spin to position it himself in dread of black.

What should have been a brave experiment deteriorates into farce. And it is to this that I took offense.

As you can see, comprehension suffers much from shoddy criticism, and collective opinion of the novel is in dire need of adjustment. Guilt and Redemption? Well, yes, but in a manner, if I may say so, remarkably different from what is conventionally espoused. *C&P*, contrary to consensus, is a study of the rash, no, the *psychotic* ways in which a person may alleviate or eliminate doubt out of despair for its *accuracy*. It is one man's battle for God, and when it becomes apparent that God is in no hurry to fight back, because, perhaps, *he cannot*, then it becomes an exercise in a most extreme form of rationalization. The conclusion, no, the *moral*: it is better to believe than to doubt, or, 'tis better to love the lost than to love nothing at all. The Author, in an uncharacteristic moment of weakness, advocates being *lukewarm*. He would correct that in a later book.

I must tell you, the thought shook me as it came to me. It wrote itself, as the saying goes among dilettantes. Yet it did! I wondered: what if God had been given the *proper* chance to speak, that is, as much time as He damned well pleased to pass judgment one way or the other? What if Raskolnikov had *actually* experimented instead of wagered, and had carried it out to its conclusion, with neither hope nor expectation? What if he had had the strength to force the moment, etc., without meddling, without *fearing* it in the name of Truth? What if he had made every possible effort to avoid justice, and had got away with murder *for the rest of his life*? Or, having made those same efforts, what if he had been tracked down in spite of them and *then* been shipped to Siberia? It would be God versus Superman, Infinity versus Nothingness, a final verdict and a new word!

Raskolnikov goes only halfway because he lacks fortitude, because he cheats. But what if he had experimented honestly, *disinterestedly*? What if he had lied through his teeth, "Detective, *signore*, I came home, and there she was, dead," and, following a thorough investigation, returned to Phila—that is, *Petersburg* cleared of all charges? What if he had made a point of *closing that door*? God's existence, or lack thereof, would be unraveled, and Raskolnikov would be the first to verify it, the first to leap "beyond Good and Evil!" Alas, our Rodya could not bear very much reality. Men like Raskolnikov find themselves swooning in police stations. If you cannot live up to it then you should not go around hypothesizing, no, *proclaiming* the Superman, etc.

God, I remember it all so vividly! How the idea pressed upon me that very morning while living with, but I must say it (though I regard it as a common piece of prairie fodder), *my* Antonia along the Adriatic. I remember the blue, no, *cerulean* sky coloring clear water blue with its reflection, and the soft breeze breathing a greener splendor on the trees. I searched upward, toward the balcony, for Antonia, but she had retreated to her room behind a white curtain, which rippled like the hem of her skirt in a perverted wind, and I thought of an incident two days past when I had become infuriated with a violin player for casting his shadow beneath her dress. Foolish, perhaps, but there are no accidents.

I returned again to our Rodya. Just how would it have turned out if done properly? It would be farewell with a mischief! Imagine solving the riddle of God's existence, or having the right to call yourself God! A new variable occurred to me. Why had Rodion chosen the pawnbroker for his victim? Aside from what he says, I mean, again, *subconsciously*. Because he knows that he is murdering to be punished, and if another must be sacrificed, then, since his heart is not truly murderous, he must choose a victim he considers useless, someone whose death will make the least mess and cause the least pain. Another shortcut! If you are to undertake something as prodigious as the existence of God then you must run the *greatest* risk, you must "make a mess," you must give God every chance to speak out against a deed so cruel, you must bring it as close to home as possible, then, and only then (should you escape), will you have your proof! You must kill what you love if you are to become God, sacrifice what you love or yourself—it is the cost of extraordinary knowledge, and it will not come cheaply; it has to be paid for, it has to be paid for, this *smartness*. You must, like Abraham wresting Isaac to the chopping block, confront the mystery of Faith, be reconciled to it or expose it, and you must do so *without orders from God*. But there was a Danish Philosopher, famous for his pseudonyms, whose Teleological Suspension, etc., has already beaten that horse, that old horse, to death.

How is the soup?...Good, I'm glad. And you're certain that's all you want?...Fine, but we must have a toast! O mighty poet! Thy works are not as those of other men, simply and merely great works of art, but are also like the phenomena of nature, like the sun and the sea, the stars and, etc., etc., etc...

What is left to say? Speech after long silence; indeed it is right! The insomnia of failure, finally, dissolves, and soon I shall snore with *impunity* beneath the pretty sheets of success. I dare *anyone* to read the novel without thinking of Dr. A. L. Ferrara. I shall be synonymous with the scene itself! I have stamped my name on it forever! Come to think of it, I hope that I have ruined it for everybody! My work is done. And I shall leave it in your hands when you have carried up this corpse and I have taken slumber in the quiet Earth. For I am a dying man, in more ways than one, and knowledge enormous makes a God of me. Young man, 'tis not so difficult to die.

What? No, nothing. Just the check, please. No, I'm not hungry, really...The scourge! Where was I? Ah, yes, Antonia...Suffice it to say, she was my lady, my *malady*. And I was faithful to her in my fashion, even if while alive she banished me to a second best bed. A word of advice—keep an eye on that Jane of yours, lest nature remember what was so fugitive...

My, but isn't literature a glorious thing? By means of it *anything* may be justified. It is very much like the Bible in that regard. You see, by means of it I am living proof, and by means of it I shall die an exemplar! Blame not my lute! For I do indeed have proof, take note. I am the first, and do not mind being a model of reproach in the name of Truth. I am convinced, when I consider how their little lights are spent, that human beings are not ready. They will execrate me, and, like our Rodya, continue blindly. I can do no more for them. We must call no one happy who is of mortal race, yes? But you! You have long been considered a sort of son to me, Stephen. Perhaps *you* shall tiptoe this same tightrope I have made taut beyond Good and Evil, while I, I retire to my Milan, so to speak, to drown my books. Listen carefully: seventeen years have passed since last I heard my Antonia tell me that she was mine, mine, fair, perfectly pure and good. Seventeen years since last I saw that faint half-flush, etc...And yet—*do you understand?*—God has not said a word!

Pneumonia

A young man, carrying a bag of trash, stepped out of his second-floor apartment to the balcony behind it, when—wouldn't you know?—the kitchen door closed and locked behind him.

He rifled the door in disbelief. Sure enough, it was locked. He pulled his house keys from his pocket and shook his head in resignation. "Lots of good these'll do," he thought. "How many times do you have to be told that it makes much more sense to put both sets of keys on the same chain? And even then, how hard is it to remember—two keys equal house and car, one key equals kitchen? How stupid are you? And why leave both sets in the same place? You're bound to mistake them! You know by now the back door locks as soon as it closes! You've been here long enough to know! I think sometimes maybe you *like* locking yourself out. You must. This is what, the fourth, fifth time?"

He scratched his head. "It happens. Though *most* people have windows to climb through! You think *I* get a window to climb through? Of course not. I'm lucky I get a bedroom. 350 a month! Don't get me wrong, you can't beat it, but still…If there's no window, there's no window. What good is complaining?" He looked at his watch. It was past midnight. "12:12! And I'm practically stranded! What am I supposed to do?" he asked aloud. "I have to get up very early tomorrow! Of all nights! Of all the nights!"

And he did have to get up very early tomorrow, just as he got up very early every morning. He worked as a day-camp counselor in a summer program at a local recreation center. He was responsible for a group of fifteen ten-year-old boys and girls. They depended on him.

"I can't be blamed for this," he thought. "Think about it. It happens everywhere." He gave the door a final tug. "What am I supposed to do?" He kicked it feebly. "They can't expect me to kick it down!"

Again, he was telling the truth. It was a very unusual door. It was steel and thick and resembled the entrance to a meat locker in a butcher shop. It had an enormous knob like a steering wheel. "You'd think I lived in a bank vault!" he laughed. "It's hermetically sealed!" He pondered it. "Somebody's just gonna have to let me in. I mean, I can't sleep outside, can I? Who'd want to sleep outside?"

He leaned over the wooden rail of his balcony and peered into the street. He hoped he hadn't used what was left of an already shrinking supply of good Samaritans. "There's always a shortage," he thought, gloomily, searching for a trustworthy passerby. "I have many valuables, *many* valuables in that little apartment. The wrong person and—well, you never know—I might end up locked out *and* robbed!"

He waited and watched as infrequent cars splashed traffic lights and lengthened puddles. The night air hovered damp and humid above the residue of an evening storm. "I'll appeal to their sense of rain!" he said aloud, and his prospects seemed suddenly promising.

Three tall girls moved quickly an in unison on the opposite side of the street. All three were on phones and gestured in rhythm. "Look at them," he said. "Just look!" He blew his hair from his eyes. "Too far. Too many." He dropped his chin on an open hand and pondered them out of sight. "Someone better get here soon."

He paced the length of his balcony, tilting at its side to spit. The saliva came slowly from his bottom lip, formed a tail and spermed a spiral to the street. He straightened and stared at rows of bedroom windows staring back. Air conditioners purred in the savage, midsummer night's stillness. A forgotten line from long ago quoted itself in his head. "The streets are calm tonight...Who *said* that?" He wondered, and, unable to remember, forgot it once again.

A fat man, apparently sans taste, appeared sans shirt between twin rottweilers. "That's plain awful," he said, backing hands-off from the rail. The fat man whistled *Mister Softee*, while his dogs had their way with the sidewalk. He crouched, scooped a handful of pebbles, but thought against it. "C'mon Schmitty! C'mon Carlton!" he heard the fat man sing, and returned to his post when they passed. "Sickening," he thought. "Go wherever they want. Don't even wipe it up. And the owners don't care! *They're* not gonna step in it! I could see if there wasn't a sign right there on the pole, 'For Christ's sake—clean up after your Goddamn dogs!' Think they listen?"

A raindrop smacked and splattered on his forehead. He put his hand out. "Did you feel that? Did you *feel* it? It's starting to rain! It's perfect! What you need to get inside is proper pity, and there is nothing better than pouring rain," he informed an imaginary classroom.

"You see, when it isn't raining, and, on top of that, it isn't cold, people tend—" He was cut off by the sound of a bus screeching to its usual stop. "They're always good. Buses are always good!" He played the trumpet on his top lip anxiously. A woman got off alone and jumped puddles across the street. He scrutinized her. She was short and thin and wearing a black and white uniform. "I suppose…Yes. She'll do."

"Excuse me!" he shouted.

The woman looked both ways around and finally upward.

"Hello, yes, up here!"

"Hello?" she said, using her hand as a visor.

"I need your help."

She put her head down and started walking.

"No! No walking. Why are you walking? I said I need your help."

She squinted to see his face. She looked both ways again. "What's wrong?" she asked.

"I'm locked out." He rifled his door to demonstrate. "See?" He did it again. "I was taking out the trash," he lifted a bag and held it to the side of his face, "when the door closed and locked on me. I have the wrong keys." He jingled a set of keys.

"What keys are they?"

"They're my car keys and my front door keys. I grabbed them by mistake."

"Why don't you put them all on the same chain?"

He flapped his lips. "Because I'm stupid and keep forgetting."

She shrugged. "Whatta you want me to do? You want me to go to a pay-phone?"

"Wouldn't help…I'm the only one with the keys."

"Then *what*?"

"I want you to let me in."

"But I don't have your keys!"

"I know *that*." He waited for a group of boys to pass behind her.

"I'm going," she hollered.

"No, wait!"

"I can't. I'm sorry."

"You're sorry? Don't be *sorry*! You gotta help me. You can't just leave me out here. How could you leave knowing you just left me out here?…We'll be five minutes. Not *even* five minutes." He flashed her four fingers.

She sighed loudly enough for him to hear it and understand it. "What do I gotta do?"

"I need you to come up here with my keys, then get the kitchen keys and unlock me."

"But I don't know where your kitchen keys are."

"I'm going to *tell* you. It's one key, right by the back door. Beneath the tissue box."

He could see her thinking. "I don't know," she said.

"What don't you know? If you don't help me, think about it, I'll be out here all night…In the pouring rain!…Because of you!"

"It isn't pouring," she said.

"But it will be. Soon."

"I don't know. I don't even like to—"

"I'm not crazy!" he interrupted. "I'm really locked out. Haven't you ever been locked out?"

"I'm sorry," she said. "I have to get home."

"So do I!"

"Can't you climb through a window or something?"

"Do you *see* a window or something? There is no window or something."

"What about the door? Can't you knock down the door?"

He turned to the door and pointed. "You can't see that either, can you? It's steel. And it's very thick. I'd break my shoulder." The rain began to thread itself through the eyes of the streetlights.

"Feel that?" he said, coughing. "We could have been done by now. I'll get pneumonia out here all night!"

"It's the middle of the summer," she said, matter-of-factly.

"Still!" He coughed again. "It can't be good!"

She locked her fingers in an umbrella above her head and sought to transfer the task to a stranger. None was forthcoming. Her shoulders sunk. "What do you want me to do again?" she asked.

His eyes lit up. "I want you to take my keys, come into my apartment, second floor, walk into my kitchen, get the key on the counter beside the sink, open the kitchen door and let me in. That easy."

"And that's all?"

"That I know of…Please! I'll give you fifty bucks."

"What?"

"Fifty dollars. I'll even throw it down to you right now…With the keys, of course."

"I don't want your money," she said, pleasantly. Her suspicion broke. "I'll do it," she said.

"Thank you! Thank you so much! You ready?" He dangled the keys over the rail.

"Yeah. Go ahead."

He dropped them. They went through her hands and skinned her nose.

"Good catch," he laughed.

"Shut up," she answered, picking them up.

He laughed again. "I'm sorry," he said. "What's your name? I'm Michael."

"What's that matter, *Michael*?"

"It doesn't. I'm being friendly."

"Now he's being friendly," she said aside. "I'm Laura."

"Please to meet you, Laura! Who was it wrote to Laura?"

"What?"

He thought about it. "I forget. Anyway. You're not a thief, now, are you Laurrrra?" He rolled the r's over his tongue.

"Excuse me?"

"I'm just saying, I *am* letting you into my apartment. I'm sort of helpless once you have my keys. And you already have my keys. You're just gonna come up and let me in, right?"

"Whattaya think I am? I'm not gonna *steal* anything!"

"Don't be insulted," he said. "I'm just making sure. I have to make sure."

"You're a little late for that, ain't you?" she said, showing him his keys in her palm.

He thought about it. "You're right. I got it backwards…Should have asked before I dropped them, huh?"

"Uh-huh."

"You won't snoop, right?"

"I'm not gonna snoop, either! Geez!…Though now that you mention it…" She raised the keys to her ear and danced them like puppets back and forth. "Maybe I *will* have a look around."

"No! Please! I trusted you!" He shouted, playfully.

"You hiding something, *Michael*? Hmmmm?"

"Of course not!"

"We'll see about that. Listen, it's been lovely chatting with you and all, but it's really starting to rain. You think we could get this over with?"

"I'm waiting for *you*!" he said.

"Oh! Okay. Where do I go?"

"Enter around the corner. The door next to the garage. Second floor. The kitchen's straight back. Remember, the key's right on the counter next to sink, under the tissues."

"Yeah, yeah, I heard you the first time. I'll be right there."

"Thank you so much, Laurrrra," he said. "Appreciate it."

She waved to him and disappeared around the corner. He sighed. It pleased him to know that there were still so many kind-hearted people in the world. Sure, some of them needed coaxing, some even needed bribes, but, on the whole, he found it to be generally true. It really did warm his heart. He had almost lost faith! A forgotten line from long ago quoted itself in his head. "I, too, have always depended on the kindness of strangers…Who *said* that?" He wondered, and, unable to remember, forgot it once again.

He kicked his garbage can an inch or two. "Wait a second. I can't—what is this?" He put his fists on his hips in mock indignation. "Wouldn't you know?" He kicked the garbage can again. It tipped over and uncovered an extra key beneath it. "All this time?" An extra key! I'll be damned," he said aloud. "Imagine forgetting something like that!" He picked it up and let himself into his apartment. He turned out the lights and sat in the love seat by the front door. He heard Laura climbing the stairs. He'd become quite professional about it. "Though it *is* getting a little too easy," he thought, with a mixture of boredom and melancholy. "Rejection is good for you. Every once in a while…I'm not even in the mood anymore." He thought of the three girls on three phones gesturing in rhythm. "Now *that*…" He heard her try the wrong key. "Stupid, stupid people! Why do all of them *do* that?" he thought, preparing.

Killin' Time

The morning moon had overstayed its welcome above another Sunday morning in South Philly, where a gray and black Buick was double-parked in front of Saint Matthew's Church. Two men in their late twenties or early thirties were waiting inside the car. One of them, in the passenger seat, was scanning radio stations. He looked ridiculously out of place in a tan suit and matching fedora.

"Oh! I love this song!" he said, singing along in marvelous falsetto:

> *Wouldn't it be nice if we was older?*
> *Then we wouldn't hafta wait so long.*

On the last word, he crossed his arms at his shoulders, gyrated in his seat, and gave kisses to the windshield.

"What's he talkin' 'bout, wait so long?" he asked. "Wait's he waitin' for?"

"He means marriage," The Driver said. He was a slim man disguised by a cigarette, obviously in charge, and dressed post-depression in jeans and a flannel shirt.

"Marriage?" The Passenger said. "What's marriage got to do wit anything?"

"Used to be, you had to wait till you were married before you could have sex."

"Till I was *what? Married?* Can you imagine? You name me one person who's waitin' till they're married."

The Driver shook his head, shrugging.

"You mean to tell me, I wanna bang some broad, right? I gotta give her a ring first? I gotta be... *betrothed?* Is that what this jerkoff's sayin'?"

"That's what he's sayin'," The Driver said.

"*Get* the hell outta here! Can you imagine? Say I'm wit Maria Vizi, right? And we're gettin' into it, and she's got her panties down around her ankles, and she's pantin' like she does, you know, and just as we're about to *vamoose* I gotta stop and tell her, 'I'm sorry, baby, but we ain't married yet, so we gotta stop it right here'?"

"Yep."

"*Get* the hell outta here! Then what happens? I gotta take her home and give her a kiss on the cheek and meet the family and all that other bullshit?"

"That's right."

"And you think that's hap'nin' nowadays?"

"I don't know. If it is, I ain't seen it."

"That's right you ain't seen it. 'Cause it ain't hap'nin'…I never knew that's what this jerkoff was sayin'. I used to like that song…You shouldn'ta told me."

"You're the one who asked."

"Well I shouldn't of." The Passenger cut the radio and sneered. His day was ruined. "My day is ruined," he admitted.

"You'll get over it," The Driver said.

The Passenger sniffed twice in resignation, turning his attention to the faux Medieval front of the gray, granite church. He crouched deep in his seat to see its twin spires arrowing the sky.

"You ever been in here?" he asked The Driver.

"Nope."

"I was. I used to go here. When I was little. Real nice inside. Ceiling's all painted—like the Sixteen Chapel, over in It'ly. Who was it painted that?"

"Da Vinci?"

"Yeah, Da Vinci. You should see it. This one, I mean." He pointed at the church in front of him. "They got this picture of the devil, right? And he's on his back, holdin' the Earth in his arms. Now imagine the size of that thing, cradlin' the Earth like that."

The Driver's interest was piqued. "What's he look like?" he asked.

"Who?"

"The Devil. I always wondered."

"Oh! Like a giant lizard. like Godzilla."

"Godzilla!"

"Uh-huh."

The Driver was skeptical. "I don't think so," he said.

"But listen," The Passenger continued, "that's not the point. The point is, there's this one angel, right, like, one of them archangels or somethin'? And he's shovin' this staff lookin' thing down the Devil's throat. And you can see God in the background, just sittin' there, watchin' everything from his throne like he's the boss, you know? I always used to look at that painting when I was a kid, because, if ya think about it, it's sorta like what we do."

"What is?"

"Well, we kill the snakes for the boss, so to speak.

"You said he was a lizard."

"Lizards, snakes, same difference."

"Both reptiles," The Driver agreed. "But what about rats? Rats are mammals."

"You get the idea," The Passenger said. "Think about it. You got God up there, like the boss, right? And his son—he's the underboss. Then you got the archangels. There like the made guys, you know? And then them angels nobody knows. There like the friggin' soldiers. They make sure everything's goin' accordin' to plan."

"And the Devil, he's like…all the deadbeats and whatnot," The Driver said, catching on.

"Yeah. He's *symbolic*. He's like all them people that don't ever wanna pay and always wanna get over."

"Like Ferliani?"

"Exactly," The Passenger said, satisfied. "See what I mean? We're no different. We're a couple-a angels!" They both laughed. "And the Devil?"

"Yeah?"

"He cradles the Earth."

"I see," The Driver said. "'Cept you gotta remember."

"What?"

"That God? He's only the *reputed* boss. Know what I mean?"

"Good point, good point."

The Passenger digested it all with an air of solemnity, while fixing the hair beneath his hat. "You sure he's in there?" he asked, placing it back on his head.

"Who?"

"Ferliani?"

"That depends. You know who's car we're blockin' in?"

The Passenger leaned and looked. "His?"

"Very good," The Driver said, nodding. "You're a regular wizard."

"I thought he had a van?"

"He's got both."

"He's got *both*, but can't pay *us*?

"Guess not."

"That's int'resting."

"Is it now?"

"Very int'resting. But what I wanna know is, why a guy like Ferliani—who's got all this heat on him—even go to church?"

"*Ma-rone!*" The Driver said, lifting his hands to the heavens, before using his hands to explain it all over again. "How many times we been through this? He goes here every Sunday. His brother's a priest, remember? Says the 10:00 mass? He takes his mom to see the son? Remember?"

"Yeah, I remember that much. I'm just sayin', it's strange, that's all."

"What's strange?"

"I thought you told me she couldn't understand English."

"She can't. She's a grease ball. Been in the country 82 years, can't understand a word of it."

"Then what the hell's she doin' in there, listenin' to the mass?"

"She ain't listenin' to the mass," The Driver said. "She likes to watch her son hold the chalice up, and the wafer, and all that other crap—the sign-a the cross, the genuflects, the friggin' altar boys, I don't know."

"So Ferliani's stuck, whether he likes it or not, right?"

"Yep. Asshole's gotta get her there and get her back. Old bag's half-a cripple."

"That's nice though," The Passenger said.

"What is?"

"I mean, it's a good son, who does that."

"You're serious?"

"No, I'm just sayin'. Guy takes care of his mother, that's all."

"Whatever."

The Passenger opened and closed the glove compartment. "But I been thinkin'," he said.

"'Bout what?"

"I don't know. 'Bout Ferliani…He goes to church, right?"

"Yeah?"

"And as soon as he comes out, we gotta whack him, right there on the front steps, his mother on his arm and everything."

"Those were the orders…Why?"

"Nothin'. It's just…What if, let's say, this guy's been in there prayin', right? And he's in there, and he starts with the, 'bless me O Lord for I have sinned and I'm sorry and whatnot,' and God forgives him?"

"And?"

"I'm just sayin'. He'd be all at peace with God when we killed him and we'd wind up sendin' him to Heaven. What kinda revenge is that?"

The Driver lost his cigarette smoke prematurely. "Heaven?" he asked, choking.

"Yeah, Heaven. What's wrong with that?"

The Driver smirked.

"I'm serious," The Passenger persisted. "I'm makin'…a *hypothesis*."

"You're breakin' my balls is what you're doin'."

"Nah, it's not like that…Seriously, what if we kill this guy, right, while he's in the middle of getting' head from his fifteen-year-old girlfriend in the back of his van, huh? We bust in on him, right? Bang! Put two right in his forehead. See what I mean? Then he's guaranteed to go to hell. And then you got the best revenge there is."

The Driver's disgust registered somewhere between stepping in horseshit and eating it. "That's the stupidest thing I ever heard." He spit.

"What is?"

"What you just said, that's what."

"I ain't sayin' it's gonna happen!" The Passenger said. "I'm just makin' conversation. I know there ain't no such thing…It's just philosophy."

"Since when *you* a philosopher?'

"I ain't, I'm just say—"

"Even if," The Driver began with a passion, "Even if there was such a thing, and there ain't, do you really think Ferliani's in there prayin'? No. He's in there thinkin' about makin' his next bet and getting' head from a fifteen year old girl in the back of his van and when his mother's gonna kick the bucket and how he's gonna come up wit all that money he owes us. Like makin' the sign-a the cross every once and a while's gonna get him off the hook for all that money."

"I know, but *I'm*—"

"No buts about it!"

"Take it easy," The Passenger said, turning his palms to The Driver.

"No, *you* take it easy! I don't like what I'm hearin'."

"What? It was a joke! You know me better than that! You know I'll cut his throat in the church! All this time, you don't know me by now?"

"Like he's gonna sprout wings and get a fuckin' harp and go live on some fuckin' cloud somewhere!…Ferliani?"

"I'm tellin' you, I was jokin'…What, you can't take a joke no more?"

"Goin' to Heaven," The Driver said, spitting. "Who cares so long as he's dead?"

"That's what I'm say—"

The Driver put his hand over The Passenger's mouth. "Imagine," he said, seriously, "you go back to Pigs and you tell him you didn't wanna make the hit 'cause the guy you was supposed to whack was sayin' prayers and 'makin' peace' and you didn't wanna send him to Heaven? You know what'll happen? You'd better be sayin' prayers yourself, 'cause you'd be next…And then me." He removed his hand.

"You're right! I know!" The Passenger said, gasping. "I can't believe I even thought of it. That guy on the radio, he had my head all screwed, I swear. The marriage thing and the whole bit. You know me, I don't care where he goes, so long as it ain't here and I get my money."

The Driver was skeptical. "First of all, it's *our* money. Once Pigs gives it to us. Second of all, are you sure of all that?"

"Sure, I'm sure! What?"

"You swear to God?"

The Passenger let a syllable stray, then paused. "Wait a minute. I ain't swearin' on no fuckin' God. Who the fuck is God?"

They both laughed.

"That's what I like to hear," The Driver said.

"Thought you had me, huh?"

"Got me nervous there. I'm sittin' here wondrin' where your head was at. You go fuckin' up, it's my ass, too"

"Don't worry 'bout me," The Passenger said. "Fuckin' nonsense. I never believed it, not even when I was sayin' I did…Swear on my mother! I was just, I don't know, sittin' outside the church, rememberin' the old days, and I was thinkin', that's all. It's like…*nostalgia.*"

"Ridiculous is what it is."

"Forget about it."

"I was you, I'd be embarrassed."

"Will you let it drop?"

"Heaven and Hell. Where'd you come from?"

"Forget about it!"

"Wait'll I tell the boys you were scared to shoot somebody 'cause you thought you were gonna send him to heaven!" The Driver keeled over in delight.

"I'm tellin' you, keep quiet."

He laughed harder.

"C'mon! What's it gonna take?"

He ceased abruptly. "Good question. How 'bout this? You give me a dollar, I don't talk."

"What! I'm payin' hush money for bein' stupid?"

"Yep. Stupidity tax. Now gimme my money," he held out his hand, "or they start callin' you Joey Bishop!"

"Ah, go fuck yourself." The Passenger said, pulling a wad of money wrapped in rubber bands from his pants pocket and giving a hundred dollar bill to his partner. "No more now. Ya hear?"

"My lips are sealed."

The Passenger waited, hoping to get it back. "One more thing I wanna know then," he said, losing hope.

"Wait, let me guess," The Driver said. "You wanna know if Noah really brought the male and female mosquito on the ark. Well, you're in luck. Since I happen to know he most certainly did, right after he parted the Red Sea!"

"Now why you gotta be like that? After I paid you off and everything?"

"I'm only playin'!"

"Well, cut it out. And another thing. Why is Pigs so set on killin' this guy on the steps of the church, in broad daylight, with his mother on his arm? We can get him anywhere."

"*Ma-rone!*" The Driver said, again to the heavens. "Figure it out. You're a bright boy."

The Passenger thought about it. "I'm shootin' blanks," he said, shrugging. "I got nothin'."

"No? Let me ask you somethin', that head-a-yours, is that just a hat-rack or what?…He's makin' an example of him! Think. You go killin' somebody at the church, what are you sayin' to everybody else who owes you money? You're sayin', 'you better pay,' 'cause once you go killin' at the church, you'll go killin' anywhere."

"You're right," The Passenger said, catching on. "It's like, you ain't safe, 'cause Pigs wants his money. And if you ain't got it, that's too bad. Hide at the church, visit your mom, do both at the same time, Pigs don't care. He calls us, we come see you."

"That simple," The Driver agreed. "All these priests, every five minutes, with the baskets and the envelopes, their makin' *their* money, why can't Pigs? Know what I mean?…Ferliani dies, everybody knows why and everybody gets the point and everybody pays. Understand?"

"*Gabeesh.*"

"Good."

The Passenger took a silencer from the glove compartment and attached it to a gun he had hidden is his blazer.

"Take it off," The Driver said.

"What?"

"The silencer."

"Why?"

"Pigs wants the shot heard 'round the world."

"That serious?"

"Yep."

The Passenger returned the silencer to the glove compartment and placed the gun between his legs. "What time is it?" he asked.

"10:33…Just about."

"Killin' time before killin' time, right?" The Passenger said, sliding his hands into a pair of brown leather gloves. "All's I'll say is, this message better work 'cause I can't take this Sunday morning shit no more. Don't Pigs know it's football season?…Who you like today?"

"I told ya. I gotta three-team-teaser-parlay-reverse-round-robin-straight."

"That's a lock," The Passenger said, cracking his knuckles.

"I got the inside scoop."

"No shit? From who?"

"From The Frog."

"Yeah?"

"Yeah. I was over at Mol—"

"Shhh!" The Passenger cut him off and pointed. "People."

The Driver straightened in his seat. "You sure you know what to do?"

"Of course." The Passenger put the gun in its holster. "By the way, you like my get up or what?" he asked, brushing his lapel.

"Sure. Now you look as dumb as you sound."

"Nah, you're crazy. I'm gonna start dressin' like this whenever we pull one a these from now on. It's like…I don't know. It's like, keepin' up with tradition, ya know? Like the old timers, in the movies, always dressed real nice. That's when they were real men. See what I'm sayin'? It's like, you're a parta somethin' else."

The Driver shook his head. "Whatever. Just go do as we planned and meet me like we planned so we can get the rest of our money and go back to the club for the games."

"Will do," The Passenger said, tipping his fedora and giving a wink.

Celia Shits!

Nondum amabam, et amare amabam, quaerebam quid amarem, amans amare.

—*Confess. St. August.*

Philadelphia. Christmas lately over and New Year's Day broken (if one may say so) above implacable January weather. String bands and mummers marching from Pattison Avenue to Market Street, hail, hailing that the gang's all here, and with them, happy days again. Newborn snowflakes, like perforated teardrops from the sun, nestling on numb noses or dissolving into blush. Breath visible in ice, confusing those with cigarettes, hanging a permanent fog in front of faces as if a thousand onlookers had furnaces for hearts. Wind tailspinning to the ankles, bouncing back in cyclones, casting handfuls of dust into eyes before plummeting again.

People everywhere. People crushed on both sides of Broad Street barricades, backed like bricks into row home walls, cluttered like the patients of a plague year on the steps and ledges of the Methodist Hospital, wriggling against the iron spikes of Southern's schoolyard, hoisted to the tops of mailboxes, traffic lights, each other's shoulders. People glued together in Scyllas, twelve-arming vendors at every corner in pursuit of pretzels, hot dogs, foghorns, top hats. People arguing with cops on foot, and, scarcely better, cops on horses, cops in paddy wagons and patrol cars. People popping corks, breaking bottles, relieving themselves in bottles, vomiting in side streets or right there on their shoes. People strutting, jostling, stabbing sequined umbrellas at the sky in a general infection of good cheer, hopscotching patches of ice, chanting obscenities and boasting wildly of golden, O them golden slippers. People rioting, carousing, throwing streamers, throwing punches, throwing blackened ice found frozen to the gangrenous mufflers of rooted cars. And in the middle of the street, people dressed in dazzling, mating, peacock feathers, satin and glitter suits, frilled and laced in an array of roman candle color, their faces painted as bloodshot, hung-over clowns, each one strumming a banjo or tooting the trunk of a saxophone, a music stand attached to their torso, wasting all the talent in the world without a care, and flanking a steel Megalosaurus, forty-feet long or so, which waddled on wheels like a drunken, elephantine lizard toward City Hall.

As such a morning thawed into such an afternoon, Stephen appeared on Broad Street in the center of everything, observing everything, as always, morosely, while huddled against the trunk of a tree, which served him as both a vantage and vanishing point, and whose tangled roots flirted with his foothold whenever he was bumped off balance by the current of the crowd. His hands were pressed to his stomach, and a grimace was pressed to his face in a fit of nausea, one part Absolut, one part Sartre. His insides had been hollowed-out by a New Year's Eve spent celebrating the death of a century and lamenting the birth of its new, less-promising replacement. The next one hundred years had begun without a peep from the pending apocalypse, though many had been certain of its coming, including Stephen, who secretly sought it as a kind of solution.

There was a temporary lull in the parade. A firecracker exploded in the distance, prompting three policemen to race in its direction. Two more exploded behind them. Stephen laughed. Through the branches of a dead tree, he tried in vain to penetrate the cold, uncaring sky. He stretched beneath its uniform, unanimous gray, which domed the city and all the world, feeling himself surrounded by so many worms and waiting for the world to end. He brooded over the prospects of a human race made saturate with war, its fierceness poised to ruin Hell for a collective imagination and to banish its predecessors into the catacombs of petty skirmishes. He had a foreboding of billions dead, at a time, of hemispheres halved by terror until the entire planet had caved-in and its rubble had disintegrated into a swallowing sun. The derangement of human history would, in his time, be excavated and repeated to adjectiveless degree, while his disinherited, abandoned generation culminated unconsciously, and its children fizzled out in denouement. Our fathers, viler than our grandfathers, begot us who are even viler, and we shall bring forth a progeny more degenerate still. On the eve of a century to extinct the species, as the pipes of midnight chimed and the rough beast awoke but failed to slouch, Stephen took a cup for auld lang syne, thought dismissively of Tennyson, ringing out the old, ringing in the new, and, making resolutions to fuck before the year was out, drank until oblivion remembered.

He was an open wound, a sensible emptiness; and on such an afternoon, his heart pumped perilously close to a demon hopelessness. Philadelphia's artificial atmosphere, which customarily pursued him like a shadow of a different shape, had grown aggressive at his back. "It's the rock that pushes Sisyphus," he thought, pulling a piece of paper from his pocket. Disillusion's heavy hand had cupped his throat and begun to squeeze. He imagined himself at the base of a broken guillotine, unaware of its disrepair, forever waiting for the blade to drop. He was enisled in the sea of life, entire of himself, like Crusoe amidst a continent of cannibals, and sickened by his search for her, his Maud Gonne.

She was at the root of everything, and without her Stephen was, to use a favorite word of his, deracinated. He had withheld himself from what he had read to be "vulgar satisfactions" in the name of an Ideal he actively pursued, a mixture of love begotten by despair and la belle dame *cum* merci. He wanted the sacrificial love, the transcendental love of his favorite novels, Sydney Carton, Charles Swann, Julian Sorel love; Marius Pontmercy, Will Ladislaw, Philip Carey love; Frederic Moreau, Heathcliff Earnshaw, Rupert Birkin love; Werther and Bazarov and so on and so forth love...In the meantime, he had been reduced to more imagined mistresses than Herrick, which only went so far.

Though his patience was at an end, his heart would not desist. Silence, but not submission...He learned that hope without an object *could* live and that it gasped for life within him. He desired her too deeply, and although opposite to humanity, was opposite to death as well, even if presently he longed to die. Stephen knew that she existed, *knew*, and what's more, that she searched for him as ardently as he for her. It had long been a foremost tenet of his soul that should his solitude relent, his suffering would cease. Oh! that the desert were his dwelling place, with one fair Spirit for his minister, that he might all forget the human race, and, hating no one, love but only her! His Asia would unbind him, would regenerate his Earth from an attic of Hell to a basement of Heaven, and soon. Until then, however, a slightly different tact was needed.

He concluded, after much investigation, that Cosettes and Catherine Earnshaws did not a home in Philadelphia make (and yet, he reminded himself, Gaddis's Esme was born here, or so they said). Nevertheless, Philadelphia would not call itself his home on the other side of summer. What was he that he should linger here? He'd simply stuff his dog-eared copy of *A Portrait of the Artist* (he was very fond of his first name) *As a Young Man* into a borrowed suitcase and exile himself, silently, cunningly. As inscripted on his right arm: *Homo fuge!* A pilgrimage would do him well. But what to do till winter's lease had run its date? He had decided on debauchery, on the strength of experience to send him off, on a temporary abatement of Ideals—all the better to prepare for his Beloved!

His reasons were many: How could he, after all, recognize let alone appreciate his Ideal, had he never encountered its antithesis? (The universe is founded upon a principle of change, and framing inflexible Ideals, he knew, should be avoided). And could one become a poet without first becoming man? Answer that! And would not a "vulgar satisfaction" serve only to reinforce his Idealism through the memory of its compromise? (You never know what is enough unless you know what is less than enough). And honestly, wasn't it time to end this apprenticeship? And so on and so forth. His Idealism had provided him with sanctuary from the fury and mire of human veins, and his lack of flesh was sad indeed, though he had, of course, read all the books. Stephen sighed and was once again knocked off balance by the current of the crowd.

Above him, the cold, uncaring sky had shredded into blue. Stephen shielded his eyes in salute of the sun: is it the sun that emerges, or the clouds that yield? On a piece of paper, he jotted down the question: *To answer: is ours her wedding garment, ours her shroud?* Looking up, his everlasting no, firmly grounded though it was in a center of indifference, emitted a tentative yes to a sight before him. Huddled there against the trunk of a tree, at his lowest, most abject point, the midriff of his face frozen between wool hat and scarf, Stephen descried what looked to be a veritable Venus in a furry cap. She was clapping mittens to the music in the street, pausing to smoke or to flip the earmuff of a friend whenever she had something pertinent to say. Besides the cap, she was bundled to the waist in a silver jacket. Her black hair buckled at the matching silver scarf around her neck, as Stephen traced her face in profile, noticing immediately the hollow of her cheeks. As though she drank the wind! he thought. Could this be her, at last? His Maud Gonne, teaching ignorant men most violent ways, hurling Broad Street among the great? He was, he informed himself, viewing Heaven in a trance.

He determined that her delights were dolphin-like, and showed her back above the element they lived in, while his imagination courted her upon a footbridge in the middle of Monet. Stephen studied her face fully as her friend retreated, leaving her alone at the barricade. A sadness overwhelmed it, an experienced and knowing sadness illuminated as if by a tenebrist's light. Often she cried, he knew, tremulous sobs, because she was extraordinary, and, because of this, sad. Here she was, Stephen thought, the greatness of the world in tears, his secret inviolate rose!

She was as quick and condescending as Miss Parker, as cursed and complicated as Miss Plath. She knew the good books twice over, had been through them twice, enjoyed French poetry in French, and wrote herself in *terza rima*. They would argue Rimbaud versus Baudelaire, Wordsworth versus Coleridge, read aloud from while listening to *The Kreutzer Sonata*, and play chess like Miranda and Ferdinand; in short, they would feast upon the famine of each other's soul (which is not to mention the prodigious mowing they would make).

Stephen was recalled to life. He had visions of the two of them reciting Shelley on the Spanish Steps, paying their respects to Proust at Pere Lachaise, sleeping as Tess and Angel at Stonehenge, listening below Saint Mary Woolnoth for the dead sound on the final stroke of nine. They'd be lionized by the literary lights of a generation past, would travel in packs with the expatriates of their own, who lived abroad, they'd say, to flee the madness of a perishing republic. He fantasized admission to an unknown, richer, more sophisticated world, an infiltration unseen since Gatsby's, and accomplished with one consenting Daisy by his side.

They were escape artists, shedding the straitjacket of blue-collar buffoonery to seek strange truths on unpathed waters, undreamed shores. Beyond the sunset and the baths of all the western stars, they would make an epic simile of their lives together, would reconcile themselves to Eden without apology for knowledge. All this he knew and had rehearsed for quite some time. He closed an eye and shrunk the city's skyline in his hand. Philadelphia had adhered to him like an incompatible accomplice, had become like Carthage to his destiny. Ignore me then in hell, he thought, spurning it like Aeneas sensing Rome.

Stephen's thoughts were interrupted by their inspiration—it seemed his veritable Venus was nonplussed. She had turned in reach of an earmuff, as was her wont, only this time to double clutch self-consciously. Her friend was gone, and her eyes took aim at every rash beholder passing by. Stephen's astonished heart stood in amazement. Their gazes locked, but for a moment, the most tenuous, eternal moment to be embroidered upon a patch of time, long enough for Stephen to absorb the darkness of her eyes and to compare it to the cloudless climes at float within the breath of night. She smiled and slid her slender frame between two men who stood behind her. Stephen lost sight of her and entered the fray himself, resurfacing by his cousin's side at the bottom step of Paul Samarra's Funeral Home. He located her again. She was separated from him now by little less than a fateful word.

He grabbed his cousin's shoulder and motioned him with a wave of his head to the top step of the funeral home. They pushed upward and politely through people, arriving at the doorway. A sudden roar arose beneath them. In the street, police were handcuffing a man dressed as an Indian, who, taking his role rather seriously, had sucker-punched another dressed as a Cowboy, much to the delight of the crowd.

"Her," Stephen said, pointing slyly. "Do you know her? Who is she?"

"Which one?" his cousin said, squinting, swaying in his second wind.

"With the cap? Do you see her? The black furry cap? The silver jacket?"

"*Her*?" He pointed rudely.

Stephen pushed his arm to his side. "Don't be so obvious."

"Why? What about her?"

"Do you know her?"

"I don't think so." He squinted. "Wait! You know who that is?"

"Who?"

"That's that girl, Jane…" he snapped his fingers, "Something. From 5th and…" he snapped again, "Somewhere."

"5th and Somewhere? Are you sure?"

"I think so…Yeah, that's her! Don't you remember her?"

Stephen hesitated. "No."

"Labor day? Down the shore? *Remember*?"

"No!"

"Well, that's her," his cousin concluded.

"That's *who*?"

"That's her! By the pool, remember, we were laughin'?"

"No…"

"With the rugburns?…On her back?"

"So?"

"So?" His cousin rolled his eyes. "From fuckin' on the floor?"

"From *what*?" Stephen said, stepping back as though shot.

"E-yep! Didn't even know she had them," his cousin said, and, becoming serious, "Or maybe she just didn't give a shit…Anyway, that's her. You remember?"

Stephen did. He looked closely. "That's not her!" he said. "It isn't—It can't be her!…*Is it her*?"

"E-yep! That's her alright." His cousin was amused.

"That's not her," he repeated. "Is it really her?"

"'Fraid so…What do you care?"

Stephen didn't answer.

"Seems to me, you're smitten," his cousin said. "Ha! You sure know how to pick'em! From what I hear," he whispered, "she had two or three that night! And see that other one she's with? Virgin whore. She'll do anything but that…Go figure."

Stephen frowned. His cousin held a finger in the air and spun around. "Jesus Christ! What? I'm talkin'!" He was being called by friends at the bottom step. One of them pulled a joint from behind his ear and raised it above his head. "Ah, I see," he said. "In that case, Steve, I gotta go." They shook hands. Stephen closed his eyes and kept them closed.

He remembered her. He remembered being sickened then by the betrayal of her promiscuity and sickened also to find himself excited by it, just as now. A similar ambivalence besieged him. On the floor! His weak heart sunk and sickened, though the image endured, floating fluorescently across his closed eyelids. He remembered his emotion of a moment ago, the two of them in Europe, speaking poetry, being canonized for love in pretty rooms! The despair of a night before returned. He had never thought himself so close to his Maud Gonne! She existed, he knew, but not here, not in such a pigsty, where beautiful girls went fucking to the floor and wore it for the world to see. Disgusting! She'd take the universe to bed with her! How did it go? *Tu mettrais l'univers entier dans ta ruelle…*

He was jolted by the thought and opened his eyes. People everywhere. He searched the crowd, but Jane was gone. He would remember her. Something new and not unlike hope had risen to his heart; he had beheld the path of his departure. Clinging to an unpardonable secret, and obsessed with it, Stephen remembered his resolution.

Holes in the Sky

If you are ever in Philadelphia (God help you) and for whatever reason want to visit Girard Park, you will want to notice something more than its namesake's house and statue; you will want instead to notice the trees that grow askance the bench directly to your right (provided you enter at the corner of 21st and Porter Streets). Take a seat, raise your eyes, see the way their leaves, depending, of course, on the season, permit a portion of sky to appear between them. Chances are, had you come a year ago, you would not have been alone.

Chances are, a young man, closer to eighteen than he was to sixteen, would have been seated next to you; his name was Alex, and perhaps it is still. He visited frequently to bury his head in his hands and "think things through," claiming the bench to your right as his own.

His problem, he wrote, was the difference between seeing *into* things and seeing *through* them. A delicate problem indeed. Thus, on a daily basis, at times even twice a day, Alex kept his appointment with the bench to your right and continued to look. In fact, it was he who first pointed out this "phenomenon" of the "see-through trees," taking possession also of the isle of sky they encircled, and relishing it selfishly as a "faraway, inexpressible hope." It was his "patch of blue" by day, the "black hole" in the center of his heart by night, yet it was his. He watched it extend by degrees in autumn, disappear like warmth in winter, return by degrees in spring, and signal summer. Thus the ebb and flow of a hole in the sky…

As a rule, he wandered alone, reserving his time in the park for himself. However, on this night his plans were interfered with, briefly, by the sight of friends already seated on his bench. He approached surprised, exchanging a pair of greetings and taking a peek at the sky. The trees were dead; it was the dead of winter. Their branches fenced in the blasts of wind. A single, quiet star was burning itself out beside a waning moon.

"Where were you?" one of the interlopers asked. "I told you, 'Be at my house at 10 o'clock.' What happened?" He flicked his cigarette at Alex in accusation. His name was Max. He was fat and full of himself, some said *because* he was full of himself he was fat. His topography was rare. The bulk of his body crumpled toward its center, while his shoulders arched above his ears as if his head did grow beneath them. For whatever reason, if there was a reason, he considered Alex to be his cousin, though their respective families were in no position to confirm this, having never met. "Facts are for fools," Max said, and proceeded to afford Alex the privileges due to "blood," which, as he phrased it, was "darker than water." "Well isn't it?" he asked, when corrected. If Alex needed anything, *anything,* he was to "make arrangements" with his cousin, who, in turn, would make arrangements.

"Where was I?" Alex asked in reply.

"Yeah. Where were you? I said 10 o'clock. It's midnight."

"Oh, I don't know. Going to and fro on the Earth, walking up and down on it."

"Going *where*? You hear this kid? What's wrong with this kid?" Max demanded of the trees.

"Never a straight answer," answered the other on the bench instead, when it became apparent that the trees were at a loss. "Ask him all you want, he won't answer you," he said, spitting at his shoes, likewise in accusation. His name was Trev, excerpted from his last name, which went on indefinitely. He was friend to none and all: sometimes mouse, sometimes rat. True to form, his face had all the markings of a rodent, an impression furthered by a facial tic, which caused him to sniff more than breathe. Either that, or he existed on the threshold of a sneezing fit, which, should it come, would go on indefinitely.

"Do you really care where I was, Trev?" Alex asked.

"Not really," Trev squeaked, in a voice consistent with his face. "But if you say 10 you should mean 10. How'd you know we were here?"

"I didn't."

"Then how'd you find us?"

"I told you. I was walking to and fro—"

"Yeah, yeah, I know. Never a straight answer." Trev spit again at his shoes.

"Why are *you* here?" Alex asked.

"I don't know," Trev said. "Nothin' else to do."

"I see. I missed a lot."

"That's not the point. You should mean what you say."

"I'll make a note of that. Listen, you think we could change benches?"

"Why what's wrong with this one?"

"Nothing. I'd just rather be on another bench."

"Why?"

"Trev, Trev, Trev," Alex said with a flourish, "reason not the need."

Trev looked at Max. "What's he talkin' about?"

"I don't know. But I know *I* ain't movin', that's for sure."

"You mean you *can't* move, that's for sure."

Max scowled. "I'll let that slide," he said, handing Alex a beer. "Really, where were you?"

"Nowhere. Home."

"All this time?"

"Yes."

"Doin' what?"

"Nothing."

"Somethin'?"

"I was reading," Alex said, turning to Trev. "Did you hear me? I said I was reading."

"Good for you," Trev said, hostilely. "Friday night, he's reading."

"What about?" Max asked.

"Nothing. Just some book. Where is everybody?"

"Some party down Second Street."

"Why aren't you there?"

"*Me?* You think I'm gonna party with a buncha harps?"

"Aren't you Irish?"

"Two percent! Only two percent, that's all!"

"Really, it doesn't matter to me if—"

"Gotta remind me!" Max said. His despair was total. "Everyday I live, the regret I feel! I'll never be made!"

"I'm sorry, Max."

"It haunts me, Al. Everyday. Who knows my regret?"

"Your last name is Quinn," Trev reminded him.

"So?"

"So you're Irish!"

"Abate! Abate was my mother's maiden name! I go by that! It don't count when you go by that."

"Who said?"

"Trust me. Everybody knows."

"What are you talkin' about? There's no way in the world you're—"

"Change the subject," Max said, sticking his hand in Trev's face. "Nobody knows how I live. The responsibilities I have. Change the subject. Quick! Alex, what's the book about?"

"What book?"

"The book you were readin'. Before you came out."

"Does he have to?" Trev said.

"Shut up. Yes. Go ahead, Al, tell us."

"I told you, it was just some book."

"I know it was 'just some book.' What book?"

"Nothing. Just some book about—"

"Here it goes," Trev interrupted. "Can't I just enjoy myself for once? Every night, it's the same thing. Nobody cares."

"Drink and shut up," Max said in defense of his cousin.

"I don't do this *every night*," Alex said, kicking a stone at his feet. "At least not to you."

"Thank God."

"Trev, I'm serious," Max said, forming a fist. "If you know what's good for you. There's nothin' wrong with reading. I read the paper everyday. And not just the sports section either!…Sometimes I check *Marmaduke*."

"I'm not talkin' about the paper," Trev said. "I'm talkin' about the books *he* reads."

"There's nothing wrong with the books I read."

"There is too! You read them, then you come out here and you bore us all to death with the details. Like we care. You think just because you care the whole world's gotta care. Guess what, it don't."

"Well, *I* care," Max said. "Forget about him, Al. Tell me."

"Never mind,"

"No, seriously, I wanna know."

"I refuse to bore Trev to death with the details," Alex said with dignity.

"Little late for that," Trev answered.

"You know what?" Max said to Trev, "You're a piece-a-work, kid. You know that?"

"Kid," Trev said, rolling his eyes. "What is it all of a sudden with 'kid'? What mob movie'd you hear that in?"

Max ignored him. "C'mon, Al, spit it out. I know you wanna talk about it. You *always* wanna talk about it."

"No I don't!" Alex said. "What's the big deal?"

"That's what *I* wanna know," Trev said. "Let it drop."

"I agree. Let it drop. You don't really care anyway."

"I do too," Max said. "And it don't matter what Trev thinks. C'mon…Give us the title."

"*The Possessed*," Alex blurted out as though it pained him. "There. You happy? It's called *The Possessed*."

"The *What*?"

"*The Possessed*, Trev."

"Whatever."

"Whattaya mean, 'possessed'?" Max asked. "You mean like…*The Exorcist*?"

"No."

"You mean like the new exorcist they're comin' out with?"

"Which one is that?"

"Where the lady hires the devil to get the priest out of her son!"

Alex groaned.

"C'mon, it's funny! Ask Trev, he knows all about it. Don't ya, altar boy?"

"Me? You're the one whose uncle's a priest. Didn't you tell us he used to give you a bath when you were a kid?"

"I never said that!"

"Yes you did."

"I did not."

"You did too! Last week."

"Change the subject! *Change the subject!* Quick, Alex! The book. What's it about?"

"I'd rather no—"

"Say it!"

Alex thought of the simplest way to say it. "It's about…Russian Revolutionaries. In the 1800s."

"See what I mean?" Trev shouted. "The 1800s! What could be interesting in that? A buncha Russians from the 1800s? I don't get it…How long is this book?"

"50,000 pages."

"*50,000*? And you're reading it! Are you crazy? Why don't you just rent the movie like Max? What's the movie, like, 10 hours long or somethin'? I'd kill myself. I really would. Or I'd die of boredom. One or the other."

"But what are they possessed by?" Max asked. "You never told us."

"Nothing."

"Then tell me this," Trev continued. "These dead Russian guys, whatta they do for me? Maybe if you told us that, we'd give a shit."

Alex ran his hands through hair. "Trev, I nev—"

"Cops!"

Trev and Max placed their bottles at their feet, looking to Alex, who was facing the street, for a sign. Alex watched through a rotted hedgerow as the car slowly drove by. "They're gone," he said.

"Like I was saying," Max cleared his throat. "I'm into history."

"You!" Trev laughed.

"Yeah, me. You'd be surprised. I dabble in all sorts-a things." He turned to Alex, "Who wrote this book?"

"You don't know?"

"Of course he don't know!"

"Was it Mario Puzo?"

"No."

"Then of course I don't know," Max said.

Alex laughed. "It's by Dostoevsky. He—"

"Listen to that *name*!" Trev shouted again. "How could you read a book by a guy whose *name* you can't even pronounce?"

"I just pronounced it, *Trevellianosantosino*!"

Max spit out his beer. "Ha! That was good! That was a good one. Trevelliano…santo…whatever. Didn't I tell you? Tryn' to outsmart my cousin! He's smarter than all-a-yous!" He raised his voice to include a couple walking toward the center of the park.

"I'm going to the store," Trev said, defeated.

"For what?"

"For I don't know. Anything's better than this. Dosdruvesky! Who the *fuck* cares? It's Friday night. Let's get some girls or somethin'."

"You find'em and bring'em back," Max said.

"I find'em they're mine."

"Yeah, good luck."

"Fuck you," Trev mumbled. "*Fat fuck*."

Max put his hand on his heart, startled. "What'd he just say? Did he just call?…He just called me that word, didn't he? Trev, look, I been givin' it a lotta thought, and I decided I'm gonna let that slide, but only this once, and only because—"

"And see ya later, *Shakespeare*," Trev said, turning to Alex, who was silent, having long ago become used to it.

"Thank God he's gone," Max said as Trev exited the park. "The rat bastid. Kid gives me *agita*. I ever tell you 'bout that time I showed him a pound of weed I was tryin' to sell? He sniffed it and said, 'That's nice, Max, but what're you gonna do wit all that spinach?' I swear to God, Al. The kid thought it was spinach!…Rat bastid. I shoulda whacked him when I had the chance."

"When was that?"

"Never mind. The regret I feel. Change the subject! Quick, this book. Tell me about it."

"Forget it," Alex said.

"No, no! I want you to tell me. We're family!"

"Why are you so set on getting me to talk about this book tonight?"

"I don't know," Max said, taking a sip of beer, "you're good at it, I guess. And I'm drunk. I like the deep stuff when I'm drunk. Like, did you know that a chicken will eat no matter how many times you feed it, until its belly explodes? It's true. Or if you pee your name in the snow, it's still your handwriting? Think about it. You'd be surprised some of the things I know…I almost passed Hist'ry in high school."

Alex thought about it. "Max, what do chickens have to do with passing history?…And aren't you *still in*—"

"Don't say it! It's too painful. No one knows how I live. Quick, tell me about the book!"

"Do I have to?"

"Yes!"

"All right," Alex said, thinking of where to begin. "Do you know what the word nihilism means? Of course you don't."

"So far so good," Max said, rubbing his chin. "Continue."

"It means…It's when you don't believe in anything."

"Like, when you don't believe in nothin'?"

"Yes, nothing."

"Nothin' at all?"

"No."

"What kinda books you readin', Al?"

"Just listen," Alex said.

"My fault…But I don't get it. If you don't believe in nothin', then ain't that a belief in somethin'?"

"No."

"Why not?"

Alex was momentarily stumped. "Because you don't *say* you don't believe in nothing, you just don't believe in nothing." Christ, I'm talking like them, he thought. "It's subconscious. Or it becomes subconscious. It develops over time. The feeling just is. You don't believe that you don't believe in nothing."

"You lost me," Max said. "What's the point?"

"The point is there's this character," Alex said, hating himself for what he was reduced to. "There's a character named Kirilov," he began again, sighing, "who has this theory on God."

"Ah, it's one of them books!"

"One of what books?"

"One of them, 'There-ain't-no-God' books."

"No, it's not. The author believed in God. His characters don't."

"Kirnov?"

"Kirilov."

"He don't believe in God?"

"It's complicated."

"How don't he believe in God?"

"Because if you think about it—"

"You ain't *supposed* to think about it."

"Forget it…The cops are coming." They hid the evidence. This time a spotlight was flashed in the park.

"Everything all right in there?" the cop asked from behind the glare.

"Everything's fine. We're only talking," Alex answered.

"Not drinkin' are yous?"

"Nope."

"Good. Just keep it down. We got some calls."

"We will." The car pulled away. Max exhaled. "Whattaya call an Italian cop?"

"What?"

"A guinea pig!"

Alex laughed.

"You like that, don't ya?…Wrote it myself."

"It's very funny, Max. Now listen. You're always asking me if you could *do something* for me, right?"

"Are you nuts? You're my *cujean*. Whatever you want, we'll make arrangements. You know what they say—blood's darker than water, right?"

"Yes. Well, I've thought of something you could do…A favor."

"Favor?" Max's eyes lit up. He waved Alex in closer. "Is it Trev?" he asked in a whisper. "Just say the word. It'll be taken care of by morning. I'll tie him to a tree…Backwards."

Alex backed away. "It isn't *Trev*! Do you really think I care about Trev?"

"I'll concrete block his sneakers and toss him in the Schyulkill."

"Max, I really just want—"

"I'll shoot him, his brother, leave the gun, take the cannolis."

"Will you stop?" Alex said, laughing. "It has nothing to do with Trev. I wanna tell you about this character…in this book I'm reading, and I want you to listen to it. That's all."

"That's all?"

"Yeah."

"And afterward? We plan a hit on Trev?"

"Sure."

"Good. Talk all you want then, kid."

Alex took a deep breath before starting. "One thing, though, you have to promise me," he said. "No interruptions. I don't care if you understand. I don't care if you agree. I just want to say it, to you, to somebody, because…If I don't…I can't get it out of my head. I read it over and over again. And I just need you to listen. That's all. Maybe that'll help. I'm gonna try, because…By tellin' you, I'm gonna try…This theory, I mean. I want you to *know* something…Just listen, okay? Without interrupting me. Please? That's the favor. No interruptions. Just let me get it out of my system, okay?"

"Sounds serious," Max said. "I need a smoke for this." Max adjusted one of his shoulders and took a cigarette from behind his ear. "Helps me think," he said, lighting it. "I like to smoke when I'm doin' business. Like when I'm at sit-downs, that sorta thing. Though it's usually cigars. You want another beer or what?"

"Yes."

Max handed Alex a bottle from the brown paper bag at his feet. "So go ahead," he said, blowing circles of smoke.

"You sure?"

"I'm smokin' my cigarette, ain't I?"

"Okay…Well. There's this character, like I said, named Kirilov, who has this theory of God, and I'm convinced you have to contend with it if—"

"*Me?*"

"No. Everybody."

"Even me?"

"Yes, listen!"

"My fault."

"Kirilov says that without God, we are all gods, only we don't know it, and that it's his duty to prove it."

"Whose duty?"

"Kirilov's!"

"Oh."

"He says, in order to be God, you have to have unlimited will, but what keeps us from having unlimited will is our fear of death."

Max raised an eyebrow, and was lost.

"Wait. Bear with me...If there's no God, the Kirilov—"

"There's a fuckin' God, Al, shut up," someone shouted, entering the park.

"Harry!" Max cheered. He was off the hook. "How ya doin', kid?"

"You know, you know," Harry said, shaking hands and accepting a beer. "Ran in to Trev."

"Where?"

"At the store."

"He tell you he almost got shot?"

"By who?"

"By me, that's who. Remember when Testa got blown up? Across the street?" He pointed to one of the houses behind them. "Trev's next."

"He didn't mention it," Harry said.

"'Cause he don't know...What'd he say?"

"Nothin'. He told me Alex was in here teachin' English again." He patted Alex on the back. Harry was tall and thin, with long, blond hair parted down the center of his scalp and pushed behind his ears. He was good-looking, successful and smart, albeit, at least to Alex, in a shallow, unimpressive way. Among friends, he was infallible, among enemies envied, and with good reason: he was earmarked for happiness, made to sport mindlessly with Amaryllis in the shade; he was *prospective*. Whenever Harry was around, Alex felt like Hamlet at the feet of Fortinbras, like Gregor Samsa following an especially long night of uneasy dreams.

"What's he babblin' about tonight?" Harry asked Max.

"Oh nothing. Green fields. What I always do," Alex answered for him.

"Huh?"

"You know, Falstaff? Henry the IV?"

"What's that have to do with God?"

"Everything."

"He wasn't babblin'," Max interrupted. "It was just startin' to get intresting."

"Was it really?"

"Yeah it was...He was tellin' me about this guy, right? And one day, out of nowhere, he goes crazy, and starts thinkin' there ain't no God, right? So he wants to show these people that *he's* God, 'cause everybody else is afraid of their free will and dies. Ain't that right?" He turned to Alex.

"Not at all."

"Then you got it all twisted, kid. 'Cause that's what you said."

"That's not what I said!"

"Whattaya mean, that's not what you said? I just sat here and heard ya say it."

"Doesn't make much sense," Harry huffed.

"'Cause it ain't what I said!" Alex screamed.

"Whoa, take it easy!"

"I never said he went crazy. Max invented that. I never said...you know what, forget it. I don't even care anymore."

"All I meant was that he had to go crazy, sayin' there ain't no God," Max said. "Everybody knows there's a God."

"Is that so? You're sure of that?"

Max clapped his shoulders in a shrug. "You tell him, Har. I gotta piss."

"I just *did* tell him," Harry said. "There's a fuckin' God, Al, shut the fuck up."

Max forklifted himself off the bench. "Uh! My friggin' leg's asleep!" he said, limping behind a tree.

"Can you blame it?" Harry said. "All that weight it has to lug around. It's fuckin' tired."

"Don't start!" Max said. "I told you about what the doctor said. I got a condition."

"Yeah, it's called you're fat."

"If only you knew what it's like! The things I deal with! That's the problem with yous kids today. No respect. When I was your age, this thing of ours had meaning. Now what? It hurts me to think about it. Change the subject! It ain't right, me showin' my softer side in public like this." He undid his belt and commenced to piss on his shoes.

"So, Har. Let me ask you somethin'," Alex said, changing the subject.

"What?"

"I'm just curious."

"What?"

"Well. You come in here tonight, you don't even know what we're talkin' about, and already you start with the 'Shut the fuck up, Al. There's a fuckin' God, Al,' and I've always wondered, Har, but who the fuck are you?"

"Excuse me?"

"It's a simple question."

"Who the fuck am *I*?"

"The one with all the answers, right? Well then, tell us, 'cause I'm fuckin' sick of hearin' it." Alex was flushed, lightheaded, his heart raced.

Harry laughed. "Is he serious?" he called to Max, who was still close to the conversation, involved in the painstaking process of tucking in his shirt.

"I think so," Max answered.

"I'm very serious," Alex said. "I want an answer...'Cause I hear it every night, and it sickens me...*You* sicken me. I wanna know. How's it feel to be *so goddamn wrong* about everything?"

"Who says I'm wrong?"

"I just did."

"Anybody, beer?" Max asked, returning. "Al, you?"

"No, you just gave me one."

"So? What are you nursin' tonight?" Max cupped his hands over his mouth as if speaking over an intercom. "Nurse Alex to the operating room, nurse Alex."

Alex ignored him, waiting for Harry, who was sipping his beer. "First of all," Harry said, wiping his mouth, "it isn't."

"Isn't what?"

"Wrong."

"How do you know?"

"'Cause I know. It's been around for a reason, hasn't it?" Harry picked up a stone and threw it. "It's like this, Al," he continued. "Every time I see you, it's the same spiel, 'There ain't no God,' 'Life has no meaning.' You're a wet blanket. And on top of that, you're wastin' your time. So like I said, there's a fuckin' God, Al, get over it. Trust me, you'll be a lot happier."

Alex gestured in disgust. "You haven't told me anything."

"I told you all you need to know."

"Which is what?"

Harry rolled his eyes. "That there's a fuckin' God! Now move on!"

"That simple, huh?"

"Works for me," Harry shrugged. "And even if it ain't, what's the difference?"

"A big difference."

"Like what?"

"Like doing things for a reason and doing things at random."

"And that's a problem?"

"Yes that's a problem!"

"Why? Do I need a *reason* to make money? Do I need a reason to get laid? Random pussy, Al, that's a good thing! And if there ain't no God, then there's always money, right?"

"That's what *I* told him," Max echoed. "Kid didn't wanna listen."

"Money and God," Harry said. "You see what I mean? I'll have both, which is why I'll be happy." He winked at Max.

"What you don't understand," Alex said, softly, against his will, "that all the money in the world is useless if in the end it comes to nothing."

"If *what* comes to nothing?"

"If *life* comes to nothing!"

"Is that right? Tell me, what book you read that in? 'Cause the way I see it, if it comes to nothin' then you might as well start livin' it up instead of worryin' about the fact that it comes to nothin'...Ain't that right, Max?"

"I already said all this," Max said.

"Fine," Alex said, taking a deep breath, "But can you imagine a world without money?"

"Impossible," Harry answered.

"That's what I mean! That's how I feel when I imagine a world without God."

"Then don't imagine it."

"I can't help it. I have to."

"Then whattaya want me to do about it?"

"Nothing. I just...Forget it. I'm sick...I just...Don't you just think you owe it to yourself to know...or...to at least search for the truth, even if—"

"Truth is, Al, I don't care. And nobody cares. So just drink." Harry took a sip of his own.

"That's it? Nobody cares, just drink?"

"That's my motto. I got enough problems as it is. Why I gotta worry about God's?"

"Because it matters," Alex mumbled. "Because whether you think so or not, all of it matters."

"I don't think so. I mean, look at you. You said it yourself, you're making yourself sick. Not me. Didn't anybody ever tell you? You're supposed to do whatever you want, and then when you're dyin', all you gotta do is say you're sorry, and you're good…Just in case, you know?…That's my plan, anyway."

"That's a good idea," Max said, rubbing his chin. "I think I'm gonna try that. Where'd you say you heard—"

"And if you're wrong?" Alex interrupted. "And you're entire life has been a lie?"

Harry shrugged. "Fuck do I care? I'll never know."

"That's exactly my point!…Doesn't the thought—of eternity—of nothingness for eternity—Doesn't the thought make your head spin?"

"Sure it does! When you think about it. It's a crazy idea…Just like, I don't know, bein' able to fly or somethin'…You think about it, but that doesn't mean it's *true*."

Alex gave up.

"I'll tell you what," Harry said. "When you die, me and Max'll meet you up there, show you around, you know, tell you we told ya so…How's that?"

Alex looked into his trees, what was left of them, and was silent.

"Hold on! I got an even better idea. We'll bet right now there's a God! Twenty bucks! We'll collect in Heaven!"

"*That's* an idea," Max said, extending his hand. "I want in on that! I'm a sucker for the action."

"Whattaya say, Al? Twenty bucks?"

"Let's make it fifty, Har," Max said. "This is a lock."

"Fine. Fif—"

"Cops!"

Alex looked over his shoulder at the approaching car. "Goodbye," he said, heading toward the exit. "I'll be sure to write all of this down," he said to Harry. "You can read it tomorrow. And the rest of your fucking life."

"Al, where ya goin'?" Max called in a hushed voice. "You're gonna get us all pinched!" Alex ignored him.

"Your cousin's got problems," he overheard behind him. "Is all your family this fucked up?" And, "Hey, Al, if you see Trev, tell him…" He blocked it out.

It had always been and would always be just like that. And one way or another, he would make them acknowledge the idiocy he despised in them, and the lengths to which it drove him. He remembered that moment, the moment of renunciation—the most exhilarating of his life!—when God was wrenched from consciousness and consciousness began anew. Prior to that moment, he had been devout, more so than his time and place suspected, falling asleep while saying decades of the rosary, going to confession behind the backs of friends, until, the more he read and thought and experienced, the less sense it made. Soon thereafter, his devotion ceased, along with thoughts that begged permission and then forgiveness for being thought. He was free and felt invincible. He sinned as a sort of revenge, until, the more he read and thought and experienced, the less gratifying it became. What was the point of God *or* Godlessness? He filled his notebooks trying to answer, spent hours at a time beneath his trees to no avail. As a last resort, he countered with faith in Art and Literature, in beauty that defied death and rebelled against life, but knew it wasn't enough. He asked himself, "Why write, if praise came posthumously? Why write, if praise is useless in the grave? And if a shred of recognition reached you while alive? What good will it do you when you're dead?" He thought of Joyce, blind and ulcerated on his deathbed. Was it enough that he had written *Ulysses*? Was he comforted by the thought? He wasn't! Joyce lived, Joyce wrote *Ulysses*, Joyce died. Good for him! What did it matter if the book kept the professors occupied? He was dead! And the book, too, would die—in time. Nothing, not even God, could outlast eternity.

The thoughts formed slowly, persistently. He thought it destiny when he stumbled upon a copy of *The Myth of Sisyphus* in a used bookstore. He took it home and prayed to it for salvation. It helped him less than it had its previous owner. Regardless of how much he wanted to, he could not possibly imagine Sisyphus happy, and the conclusion that nothing mattered grew into something instinctive, as did his outrage at the faithful, who were everywhere and lying to themselves and laughing at him—at him!—because he knew better. If only he had someone with whom he could commiserate! He'd suffer peacefully, even find a way to be amused by his suffering. But there was no one here who understood, no one here who had ever read a book *by choice*, no one here who had ever been kept awake and baffled by the thought of God and Death. How could they not? He asked himself over and over, *how could they not?* The thought of an eternal nonexistence made him faint, the thought of God made him angry, and the thought of life spent pushing toward either made him sick. Then, referred by Camus, he picked up *The Possessed*, searching for Kirilov, afraid that he had found his answer. Now he was sure. It never occurred to him that his patch of sky extended far beyond Philadelphia. It only occurred to him that he could not wait for its return to signal summer. He would establish his free will, confirm his unbelief. There was another, more serious hole in the sky.

He entered his house. It was quiet, excepted for his father's snoring. "Thank God," he said to himself. Earlier that evening, his father and his father's girlfriend had fought each other throughout the house. As always, he had plugged his ears and read through it. He thought of his mother while climbing the stairs. She wouldn't have helped, nor would she have deterred him. She had spent most of her time waiting for and dreading his father. Alex opened the door to his room. Books were on the floor, under the bed, in the closet, on the nightstand. His father treated them like roaches, stepping on or over them in disgust, threatening to get rid of them if Alex didn't exterminate them himself. Some people—he reminded himself—kept books on *bookshelves*! Two, sometimes even *three fucking bookshelves*! Was that asking too much? It may have changed his mind…I'm writing that, he thought.

The increased volume of his father's snoring, and its sudden violence, traveled through the shared wall of their rooms. Alex opened his bedroom door and listened. He heard his father's girlfriend moan beneath it and understood. He cringed and closed the door. A thought recurred, but was again discarded. Kirilov would never. That was not what this was for. This was to prove that he was free, not only *of* God, but *as* God, and, most importantly, that he was free of all them. But wasn't Kirilov's goal to teach man how to *live*? Alex struggled with this, concluding, in the end, that a place like Philadelphia precluded life. Besides, Kirilov was a fiction; by doing this he would make him fact. He took his clothes off, and a piece of paper from a folder on the floor. He drew a face with its tongue sticking out.

How Quietly and Gently...

"But these are all lies: men have died from time to time, and worms have eaten them, but not for love."

—*As You Like It.*

He found its pages pinned to the bathroom door. They read:

૦૭

Tristan,

I am dead. Open the door. Slowly. Prepare yourself. And please, whatever you do, don't make a scene! And don't be sad. No longer mourn for me...It's your turn now.

He opened the door. Slowly. She was smiling. Her clothes were rolled in a ball beneath the sink, a needle and belt were on the toilet seat, a razor was balanced on a thin piece of soap. "Sharon," he said quietly, shaking her gently. Beneath the faucet, red water hiccupped. "What the fuck?" he asked her, shutting her eyelids and closing her mouth. It opened again and smiled. He turned her face to the wall's green and yellow tiles and continued reading:

૦૭

...It's your turn now.

You didn't think I was lying, did you? No. It's occurred to me that if we are going to speak, then we should do so with conviction. What's the line you are always saying? "Words are for those with promises to keep"? Well, I've kept mine. All those nights in bed, talking. Were you only talking? And don't you dare blame this on the fucking drugs! I am NOT fucking high! I've written and rewritten this for weeks, entirely straight. I know exactly what I'm doing. What about you? Was it just the fucking drugs? I don't believe it. I wouldn't have done it otherwise. I believed you. I died believing you. Will you disappoint me? Of course you won't. You know as well as I it's our only choice. Besides, you knew it was coming, didn't you? I've been hinting at it, preparing you for it, I even detected your approval and anticipation…You got what you wanted. Think about it. Could we have really gone on like this when "all true love must die. Alter at the best into some lesser thing"? Honestly, look how we live! We're a landlord's leniency from the street, and you know it. What else is there to do now, but "die of love and lengthen it"? Those are your words. Do you remember them? You'd be surprised how much of you I've retained—as fucking high as you think I am. You were always a kind of Abelard to me. Most of the time I'd provoke you, breech the subject to see where you stood, each time gauging whether or not I could trust you. And when I decided I could…Well, here we are. You've been more than sympathetic toward the idea, you know, and have said quite a lot in support of it. Fool that I am, I took you literally. But am I a fool? And was it a mistake? Need I remind you that life without me is "instantaneous Gethsemane," the ground beneath your feet "as Golgotha," your heart "Gehenna's chopping block"? Sound familiar? You said that you would, "love me to death." That's not enough. It's been said by lesser men than you. I want proof. You said that you would "sacrifice anything for me." Well, then, sacrifice your love! I want a knight of faith, not an addict of empty words. Your bluff has been called, my love: will we or will we not have this Lie-bestod of yours? For months now, you've been begging me for an answer, for a "solution" to life. Here it is. Do you remember when we sneaked into the Art Museum to "roam around in the Middle Ages"? You said that medieval artists, judging by their obsessive variations on the theme, must have taken a perverse pleasure in crucifying Christ. You said there were two faces of crucifixion: the first a face of arrogance, as if Jesus were saying, "O what fools these mortals be!" painted by an artist whose faith was unquestioned, while the other, the truer of the two, was a face of anguish and despair, of disbelief in resurrection, created by an artist who painted his own doubt upon the face of Christ. You said that for these artists, the act of painting was an act of contrition, a way to alleviate and atone for their secret skepticism, and that their art was a way of "protesting too much." You said that they rebelled against uncertainty by painting more powerful prayers. Then you asked, "Where is our alleviation? For what do we atone? And what is our prayer? To what should we offer penance, if there is nothing left to doubt?" You said that we have not lost faith, but rather our desire to doubt, that we have been reconciled to nothing on a "pilgrimage to no discernible shrine." For emphasis, we visited to the 20th century, only to find inverted urinals and bicycle wheels. Do you remember? On the steps, we decided to have faith in each other, since the world had " really neither joy, nor love, nor light." We descended and swore before the "Shakespeare statue," and I told you not to swear at all except by your gracious self, and I'd believe you. And though it all sounded very nice, I must admit, that even then it bothered me. It's an old idea. So I thought about it, and as I did began to wonder, were we merely players or were we speaking the truth? It was then that I decided I cannot praise "a fugitive and cloistered faith," since every vendor on the street below us, who fancies himself in love, can say that he would die for his "beloved." But not you. You're a "poet," are you not? You are Tristan, yes? Then why do you insult me by describing your love with their words? Enough words. Especially "love." It is too often profaned. I want the act itself, the most faithful act of all from you, or it's betrayal. Don't you see? All love dies except the love that kills itself. All love dies unless extinguished at its most intense. Prove that they lie—or that you do. Will our deaths be tragic, or merely sad? Will it alone bring destruction or fulfillment "to our dreams and our desires"? Which will it be? If death is the only absolute, and we claim our faith in each other to be likewise "absolute," then it follows that this faith of ours must be made one with death or it is false and it is relative. The syllogism holds. Otherwise, it's your literature and not your fucking drugs that have ruined my life. Otherwise, it's true, like you've said, that we cannot be saved, and even worse, cannot be rescued. Salvation, too, is dead, and you have killed it. You asked me to save you; instead I have given you the means to save us both. If I have gone first, it is not that I can't be trusted, but because I would much rather believe in you than be believed in. I know you, and know you are just the opposite. Do you see how I consider you always? How often did you say that you are, "nothing but your word"? It was your eternal theme, your more powerful prayer. When I first met you, you made a joke of my name. Do you remember it? You called me Charon. It was appropriate. You said that if you took an oath on the river Styx, and later disgraced it, that you'd be punished with nine years of silence. I've made you swear to this. You repeated the myth. Our myth. And it is more than myth to me. Can't you see how it all becomes real if you keep your promise? I believe in them, as I believe in you, and have killed myself trusting you to follow, trusting you will kill yourself because I trusted you. That is absolute faith. If you love me to death, will sacrifice anything for me, then prove it, as I, like Senta, have proven it to you. May our bodies bear witness to our love, may our love be made commensurate with these words, and may these words, in turn, be made flesh. I love and trust you.

Yours,

Isolde

PS—I've thought of something else. Do with my body what you will, yes? I mean, beforehand. And do with yourself how you will, only, remember when I first mentioned this to you? The very first time? Explaining what it meant to go first, what

it took to go second? And you suggested a "convergence of blood" at the end?
And we agreed that it was perfect? You weren't lying, were you?

I'm waiting,
Sharon

He folded the note and put it in his pocket. Again he looked at her, at her lifeless breasts, drooping toward her armpits, at her pubic hair matted at the surface by water and blood, at the holes in her arms and the slits in her wrists. He thought of David's *Marat*, he couldn't help it. She actually went through with it! He should have known. All those questions, those insistent vows. He had thought it all a strung-out and idle threat, drug talk. Now what? And where did she get the drugs? How long had she been holding out? What kind of faith was that? It made him hate her. He thought for a moment then ran to the living room, or what was left of it—four crates, a folding chair, a broken television and a telephone. "Please be on!" he said, bringing the phone to his face. It was. He dialed, twice, steadying his hand.

"C'mon! Ple—Christine!" He sighed. "Thank God you're home. It's Christopher. Yes. Nothing. No. I need to come over. Now! I need to stay with you for a while. Yes…No, nowhere. She's right here! In the bathroom. I don't know. Please! Yes, I told her. Yes, about you. Can I please come stay with you? Just now, yes!…Please, I'll tell you when I get there…Do you have anything? How much?…Thank God. No. I'm comin' now. Yes. I love you too. Good-bye." "You hear that?" he said, hanging up, shouting at the bathroom, "There's always another girl!…You don't remember *that*, do you?"

He ran to the bedroom, or what was left of it—a mattress surrounded by clothes and crates. He kicked his clothes into a pile and heaped them into a duffel bag. He went through the pockets of Sharon's pants. Nothing. "Of course not. You fuckin' spent it all behind my back," he screamed, opening a jewelry box beneath one of the crates. *Für Elise* played. Inside, there was a single, silver earring left. He put it in his ear on his way to the bathroom, taking the needle from the toilet seat and putting it next to the note in his pocket. He swung the belt through the loops of his pants. "You fucking freak!" he shouted at her, closing the shower curtain. "I can't deal with this right now! How am I suppose to deal with the cops like this! You ever think of that? No, no, of course not!" He thought for a moment, before running back to the living room. He grabbed the phone and dialed *nine-one-one*. When the dispatcher answered he dropped the phone off the hook beside the receiver. Slinging the duffel bag over his shoulder, he exited through the bathroom window to the fire escape behind it. On the ground, he tore the note into pieces with difficulty and pushed it through the grates of a sewer. More than his hands had begun to shake. "Twisted fuckin' girl!" he said aloud, hurrying toward the middle of the Italian Market. "Too many books. I told her."

Fruit and vegetable stands lined the streets, submerged in people, each willing to die for their beloved. He inhaled the market's atmosphere of rotting fish. "God, that's awful," he thought, holding his breath, quickening his pace. "Tristan and Isolde! Even *Wagner* knew better!" He wondered, had he really said those things? He asked her to save him? When? He couldn't remember, or he remembered vaguely. It all must have been a strung-out and idle promise, drug talk. Either way, what kind of a sick fucking girl would take him seriously? Half of it he'd been saying since high school! Instantaneous Gethsemane...God forbid. He felt sick. What did she write? "Nothing left to doubt. Desire to doubt." He was only stating *the fucking facts!* All those vows she made him—"Jesus Christ, that's *awful!*" he said, interrupting himself. The odor of fish grew stronger, emanated from everything and everywhere, filled his lungs each time he gasped for air until, finally, it overpowered him. He was nearly running when he stopped himself. *"Fucking words,"* he said, vomiting.

0-595-31819-3